THE BOYFRIEND
EXPERIENCE

NEW YORK TIMES BESTSELLING AUTHORS
Carly Phillips
Erika Wilde

Cover Design: Melissa Gill Designs
Formatting: BB eBooks

He's the total package.

Except . . .

Eric Miller isn't looking for a long term relationship. And he definitely isn't thrilled when a friend signs him up for The Boyfriend Experience app behind his back. It's not like he has a problem getting women on his own. But when he gets a notification that someone is in need of his . . . services, he's intrigued enough to check out her profile and can't resist the sexy, sassy little brunette who only wants him as a decoy for a family event.

Evie Bennett needs a boyfriend, stat. Someone who can accompany her to her family reunion so she doesn't have to explain that she's been recently dumped. Again. She's perfectly happy being an independent woman, but what's a girl to do when her new fake boyfriend starts to feel like the real deal?

CHAPTER ONE

"DOES ANYONE KNOW a hot single guy they could set Evie up with for a weekend?"

Evie Bennett shot Jessica—her good friend and one of her business partners—a what-the-hell look, though she couldn't say she was completely shocked by Jessica's impulsive question to the women in their salon and spa since her friend had little to no filter. But seriously, Evie didn't need their clients knowing her personal business.

"Why do you need a hot single guy, Evie?" the young, twenty-something girl sitting at Jessica's nail table asked. Her name was Lacey and she was adorably ditzy and clueless. "Aren't you already dating someone?"

Ahhh, the drawbacks of working in a small, open-concept salon, where no topic was off-limits, including Evie's love life . . . or lack thereof, she thought with a grimace as she continued flat ironing her client's hair.

"*Was* dating someone," her other friend and business partner chimed in as she walked toward the reception area to greet her two o'clock facial. Scarlett was the *spa* portion of Beauty and Bliss Salon and Spa. "But he ended up being a shady, two-timing jerk."

Asshole was a more apt term, in Evie's opinion. After four months of dating Eric, she'd discovered that he'd been living a double life and she'd been his dirty little secret. And in a desperate attempt to appease his furious fiancée, he'd devastated Evie in the process with his insistence that she'd meant nothing to him. Even a month later, that embarrassing recollection and those words still stung like a fresh slap to the face.

As far as dating and relationships with men went, she couldn't seem to get it right. Her judgment when it came to their sincerity and fidelity sucked and she was clearly too easily charmed. Seriously, how had she allowed Eric to fool her so completely when she should have been more cautious and aware of all his excuses, last-minute changes of plans, and the fact that he preferred that she call before just dropping by his place?

Now she knew why. It would have been too much of a risk of her finding him with his fiancée. Instead, she'd run into the two them, hand in hand and being very affectionate, at the movie theater. He'd told her he was going out with the guys for the night, and at the last minute, Evie had decided to join Scarlett and Jessica in seeing the latest blockbuster romantic comedy. Needless to say, seeing Eric with another woman had led to a confrontation that had put a damper on the evening and left her feeling used.

"Men can be such dogs," Jessica said vehemently as she filed down her client's nails.

"I agree," the younger girl sitting across from Jessica said. "We should kidnap him and tar and feather his dick and balls."

The idea made Evie laugh and lightened her mood. Yeah, she could definitely get on board with that.

"Not *all* men are dogs," Peyton, the pretty, blonde-haired woman sitting in Evie's chair getting her hair done, interrupted. "Trust me, there are some really great guys out there."

Scarlett snorted in disbelief. "Finding a great guy these days is like trying to find a needle in a haystack. They are a rare breed."

"True," Peyton agreed with a smile. "And yes, sometimes you have to kiss a lot of trolls to find your prince, but it's so worth it."

Both Jessica and Scarlett stared at Peyton as if she was from another planet, and Evie quickly interjected, "Don't mind Peyton. She just recently married *her* prince, so she's a little biased about the whole dating scene and everyone getting their happily ever after."

"Ahhh," Jessica said, nodding in understanding. "That explains it."

Peyton blushed, and Evie met her gaze in the mirror in front of them and smiled. She wasn't best friends with Peyton, but as her client, they'd gotten to know one another fairly well. Evie had heard all about how Peyton and Leo Stone had ended up together. It was a cute story, and sort of similar to Evie's current predicament of needing a guy for a family function. Peyton had managed to persuade her college crush to fill in as her fake boyfriend for a wedding, and their attraction from years ago had evolved into love.

At the moment, Evie's heart and emotions were far too battered and bruised to even consider falling for another guy anytime soon.

"You know, I could set you up with my best

friend's older brother and you can see how that works out," Jessica's client offered enthusiastically. "He's thirty-two, very good-looking, super successful, and single."

"Good-looking and successful are definite pluses," Scarlett said, adding her two cents as she led her appointment back toward the private spa room. "You might want to consider it, Evie."

"What does he do for a living?" Jessica asked, voicing the question that Evie was wondering herself. Successful could mean anything from a lawyer to a drug dealer.

"He's an ob-gyn."

The salon went quiet, and Evie met Peyton's wide-eyed stare in the mirror, both of them telegraphing the same thought... *no fucking way.*

"Oh my God. Are you kidding me?" Jessica stopped filing the girl's nails to gape at Lacey in shock. "Nobody wants to date a guy who spends most of his day with his face and hands up in a woman's business!"

Evie and Peyton struggled not to burst out laughing, and Evie failed as a small snort managed to escape past her lips, which in turn made Peyton snicker.

"I was just trying to be helpful," Lacey said, her face scrunching up as she thought about the guy's profession. "I think that's why he's had such a hard time finding, and keeping, a girl-friend. They're all intimidated by the amount of pussy he's seen. But ob-gyns need love, too."

Evie groaned. She was so done with this conversation. "I appreciate everyone's help, but I'll be just fine. Really."

But really, she wasn't fine. Not when she was beginning to seriously question her taste in men. Eric wasn't the first guy to string her along, only to blindside her with the realization that he'd never intended for her to be anything more than a convenient side piece for him to fuck when the mood struck. Not that she was opposed to having a friend-with-benefits kind of agreement, as long as she was clued in to the terms of the relationship beforehand and the guy she was sleeping with was single.

So, while Eric's delivery might have been different than previous guys, the end result was the same. She was left feeling like crap about herself . . . and back to square one when it came to finding a decent man who wanted a commit-ted relationship with her.

"So, you never answered that girl's question," Peyton said, her voice low to keep their conversation private. "Why do you need a single guy, Evie? Is it for that Fourth of July family reunion you mentioned you're going to in a few weeks?"

"Kind of?" she replied, not sure how to explain her situation.

An understanding look passed through Peyton's eyes. "Is your family pressuring you to settle down and you want to avoid the hassle?"

Done straightening Peyton's long blonde hair, Evie finished off the style with a glossing spray that added a nice shine to her locks. "Actually, no. That's not it at all." Her reasons were more complicated and personal, and since Peyton had been through a similar scenario, she decided to confide in her.

"My parents are actually great. They're supportive and have a very open-minded approach to relationships, and they've never made me feel as though they expect me to get married at any point in my life." They were also a little eccentric and unconventional, which was a conversation for another day. "The truth is . . . I just don't want to deal with those pitiful looks and comments when my relatives find out I've been dumped. Again." That was the simple explanation to something that was far more complex.

"I might have a solution for you," Peyton said, and she must have seen the skeptical look on Evie's face, because she quickly held up a hand and added, "Hear me out. My brother-in-law, Dylan, is an app developer, and he recently created one called the Boyfriend Experience."

"Okay . . ." Evie frowned. "Is it an escort service?"

"No, nothing sordid like that," Peyton assured her with a small laugh. "It's a legit app for women who want or need a guy for a special occasion or event. There is a fee for their services, but it's not for a sexual exchange or a hookup. It's actually kind of cool because you have the ability to choose the perfect man for you, based on what you need him for."

Evie unsnapped the black hair-cutting cape secured around Peyton's neck and shook it out. "Sounds way too good to be true, but I'll admit I'm intrigued." A temporary boyfriend would go a long way in making the reunion much more bearable, not to mention, it would help her having to face yet another ex-boyfriend who'd broken up with her and was now engaged to Evie's cousin, Raquel. She wasn't looking forward to that awkward meet and greet, either.

"All of the applicants are vetted through background checks," Peyton went on, a tinge of excitement in her voice now that she'd piqued Evie's interest. "The app hasn't officially launched yet. It's in the beta testing phase, but since Dylan is my husband's brother, I'm sure I could persuade him to add you to the app now as long as you participate in the questionnaire you'll receive once the date is complete. What do you think?"

Evie thought she was crazy for seriously considering the idea, but the notion of spending a long weekend with her relatives, and her cousin, who always made her feel lacking, outweighed the embarrassment of hiring a fake boyfriend so she didn't have to deal with any drama.

As a bonus, she wouldn't have to worry about any complicated or messy emotional attachments with a hired boyfriend. Once he'd fulfilled his end of the bargain, they could go their separate ways, because Evie definitely wasn't in the market for anything serious, and especially not with a guy who was on an app that essentially made him a serial dater.

"Okay, I'll give it a try," Evie said, and hoped she didn't come to regret her decision.

BY THE TIME Evie arrived home after work, there was an email in her inbox from a Dylan Stone, owner of Stone Media, letting her know that Peyton had contacted him to ask that Evie be added to The Boyfriend Experience app. In his message, Dylan explained how the program worked since it was still in its beta stage. The men were required to provide a recent headshot and personal profiles that included their physical characteristics, personality traits, and what kind of role they were willing to take on as a boyfriend for hire.

He assured her that all the men went through a rigorous background check before being approved, and once she found someone she felt was a match for what she needed, she could ping them and discuss the details from there. All of the "boyfriends" adhered to the same flat-rate charge for an evening of their services, and any more time than that could be negotiated between both parties.

At the end of the email, Dylan provided a

link to download the beta version of the Boyfriend Experience app so she could create an account.

Needing a bit of liquid fortitude before she went on the hunt for a temporary boyfriend, Evie poured herself a tall, generous glass of wine, and with her cell phone in hand, she curled up against the corner of the couch and tucked her legs beneath her. After a few long drinks of wine, she put her glass down on the end table and started setting up her account.

Surprisingly, she was only required to input her basic personal information, along with a profile picture. No physical characteristics or personality traits necessary. Since she was essentially the customer, shopping for the perfect guy based on *her* needs, there was no reason to list her attributes. She liked that the women had all the leverage since they were the ones doing the hiring.

After uploading a recent photo for a headshot, she glanced through the search terms listed on the app to define what kind of guy she was looking for. There was arm candy, the charmer, the guy next door, businessman, bad boy . . . The list was endless. She steered clear of the bad boy and clicked on the charmer.

Next, she selected the top three character traits that were most important to her. Confidence, because he needed to be convincing enough to pull off the whole fake-boyfriend charade. Kind and considerate, because if she wanted to introduce her family to an asshole, she would have taken *the cheater* home. She skipped over passionate and romantic because she wasn't looking for a man to sweep her off her feet, and opted for a good sense of humor. He was going to need one to deal with her offbeat parents.

While she took another drink of wine, the app went to work finding matches based on her selections. Once that was done, she scrolled through the names and photos of the guys that appeared on her screen. She wasn't looking for a love match, but the first few men did nothing to stir her interest. If she was going to spend a weekend with a stranger, she wanted to make sure *she* felt some kind of attraction so they at least looked convincing as a couple.

Then she found him. Eric Miller. The fact that he had the same first name as her ex would make it easy to keep his name straight so they weren't outed. But honestly, it was his profile picture that appealed to her the most and not just because he was drop-dead gorgeous. His face, expression, and appearance summed up his personality. His dark brown hair was a little longer than what was the norm and appeared disheveled, so he clearly wasn't an uptight metro-sexual kind of guy. His eyes were stunning—a deep vivid green rimmed in gold, but it was the glimmer of amusement in their depths that conveyed that he didn't take life too seriously. And the slight, flirtatious curve to his lips was potent enough to charm the panties off of a nun.

So far, he checked off all the attributes she'd listed.

Intrigued, she clicked on the link that took her to his profile page and the bio he'd written about himself.

Looking for a temporary boyfriend for hire? Then I'm your guy. I'm friendly, outgoing, and depending on your needs, I can take on any role you require. I make an excellent wedding date and/or I can impress your boss at a business-related function with my wit and charm. I'm happy to make your ex jealous by focusing my full attention on you, until you're blushing and he's fuming. I can play the doting boyfriend and convince your family and friends that you're in a solid, committed relationship, complete with public displays of affection if requested. No matter what type of boyfriend you hire me to play, I always aim to please!

By the time Evie finished reading the blurb, she was grinning—something she hadn't done much of since her ugly breakup a month ago. The whole bio seemed very tongue-in-cheek, and there was something about this guy's humor she found appealing and irresistible. It didn't hurt that he was gorgeous and his eyes alone made her stomach flutter with awareness.

He had the potential to be exactly what she needed to make her family reunion more tolerable, and before she lost her nerve, she finished off the last of her wine and pressed the link to send him a notification that she was interested in hiring him.

CHAPTER TWO

N OW THAT ERIC'S best friend and business
partner, Leo Stone, was in the midst of
wedded bliss with his new wife, hanging out
after work didn't happen very often anymore.
But once a month, Leo and his two other off-
the-market brothers, Dylan and Aiden, made it
a point to have beers and a burger at a local
joint with Eric, just to keep their man card
intact, Leo jokingly told him.

Whatever the reason, Eric was grateful because he enjoyed the male friendship and
camaraderie, even if at times he felt like the odd
man out, being single while listening to his
friends talk about how great their significant
others were, or Aiden being completely smitten
by his adorable daughter.

But despite being the only single guy in their
group, remaining a confirmed bachelor was a
conscious choice Eric had made long ago. Not
because he was against matrimony or a commit-

ted relationship. No, his reasons went much deeper than superficial playboy tendencies, though he had no doubt that's what a lot of the women he dated pegged him as. It was easier to let them believe that than admit the truth and reveal deeper fears he'd never shared with any woman.

As they finished up their burgers, Eric's cell phone let out a ping, indicating that one of his apps had pushed through a notification. He knew it wasn't a text or call for the Prestige Car Service business he ran with Leo, but he picked up his phone and glanced at the message, just to make sure it wasn't something important.

You have a notification from the Boyfriend Experience app.

Eric frowned, momentarily confused by the notification. He knew what the Boyfriend Experience app was since Dylan had created and designed the software and had been bugging the shit out of him to be a beta tester, but Eric had flatly refused to be one of his guinea pigs. He had no problem getting women on his own, and he had zero interest in pretending to be someone's significant other for whatever the reason some random woman desired.

Eric knew, without a doubt, that at no time had he downloaded the app to his phone ... which meant that Dylan was most likely the culprit.

Pushing his empty plate to the side, Eric glanced across the table to confront said culprit. "Hey, Dylan, I just got a notification from the Boyfriend Experience app. Since you're the developer, care to tell me how the software ended up on my phone without my knowledge or permission?" Then a thought occurred to him and he narrowed his gaze. "Did you *hack* my phone?" Eric wouldn't put it past the other guy, because he was certain Dylan was computer savvy enough to do exactly that.

Dylan popped a French fry into his mouth and smirked at Eric while his brothers, Aiden and Leo, looked on with interest. "No need to get your panties in a twist, Miller. I didn't hack your phone. I'm good, but I'm not *that* good."

Eric arched a brow. "Then how did your app, the one I didn't want any part of, suddenly appear on my phone?"

"It wasn't sudden," Dylan clarified. "The program has been on your phone for a while now. I put it on there when you were my partner for trivia night. You conveniently left

17

your phone on the table while you went to the restroom, and it was an opportunity I couldn't pass up."

Eric remembered that evening . . . mostly, how neurotic Dylan had been about one-upping his current fiancée, Serena, and her then date, mostly out of jealousy. Dylan had won the trivia game and bragging rights, but it had driven a deeper wedge between him and his best girl friend. Luckily, Dylan had realized just how much he loved Serena before he'd lost her for good.

"However," Dylan went on, a devious gleam in his eyes. "I did just recently activate an account in your name, and since the app was already downloaded to your phone, that data automatically transferred to your profile, which now makes you eligible to receive requests."

Leo chuckled and shook his head. "Wow, that was kind of ballsy, Dylan."

Eric agreed and was pissed off. "What the hell would you do that for?"

The other man shrugged as he continued eating his fries. "Just a friendly payback for all the crap you gave me at trivia night. And I thought it would be fun to fuck with your head a little bit. So far, I'm enjoying myself immensely."

"You're such an asshole," Eric said, though he wasn't completely surprised that Dylan had hijacked his phone. He still hadn't looked at the app. He was honestly afraid to see what awaited him.

"Oh, for crying out loud," Dylan said dramatically. "Give me your phone. I'll take care of it."

Without thinking through the consequences, Eric unlocked the device and handed it to Dylan, with both of his brothers watching the whole scenario as they finished their beers. He thought Dylan intended to deactivate the app, but when he started typing on the phone's keyboard, Eric's suspicions were piqued.

"What are you doing?" he asked.

Dylan didn't look up from his task. "I'm taking care of it, like I said I would." His thumbs continued tapping on the screen, longer than Eric felt was necessary. When he was done, he looked up at Eric with a smartass grin.

"There, it's done," Dylan announced, much too cheerfully. "I accepted her request for you, and you're meeting her tomorrow morning at 7:30 at the Espresso Cup to discuss the details of being her temporary boyfriend. Her name is

Evie, and judging by her photo, she's pretty easy on the eyes."

Jesus Christ. Eric snatched his phone back. "You really are an asshole. How do I retract that message?"

"You can't." His friend sat back, clearly enjoying Eric's annoyance, along with both of his brothers' amusement as they quietly looked on. "It's already sent."

He swore beneath his breath. "I'm not doing this. I'm not going to be some woman's fake boyfriend."

Another ping sounded on his phone, and he reluctantly glanced down at the notification on his screen from the Boyfriend Experience app. Evie had already sent him a response.

I'll be there. I'm looking forward to meeting you. See you in the morning. She followed that up with a smiley face.

Eric groaned in defeat. What did he say to that? *Oh, sorry, I changed my mind seconds after setting up a time to meet?* He wasn't that much of a dick. He didn't know this woman, and any other guy probably wouldn't have hesitated to rescind the offer, but the thought of her feeling as though he'd personally rejected her, maybe based on her looks, wasn't his style.

"I don't see what it could hurt to meet her and hear her out," Aiden piped in. "It could end up being an interesting date. It's not like she's asking you to put a ring on her finger and marry her."

"This is so *not* my thing," he muttered.

"It wasn't my thing, either," Leo reminded him with a laugh. "But I have to admit, being Peyton's fake boyfriend was fun, and as a bonus, I got the girl."

"You *knew* Peyton," Eric pointed out. "You went to college with her and you at least had some kind of history to make the whole relationship thing look believable."

A sly smile lifted the corner of Leo's mouth. "I *dare* you to do this," his friend challenged.

"I'm going to double down on that dare," Aiden added, his tone filled with way too much amusement.

"Make it a triple," Dylan said, clearly wanting in on the bet.

Eric shook his head. Nothing like being ganged up on. "You do realize that I get nothing out of this except being used for some woman's amusement, right?"

Aiden grinned. "There are far worse ways of being taken advantage of by a member of the opposite sex."

Eric rubbed his fingers across his forehead, knowing he'd pretty much lost the battle, not because of the three dares his friends had just issued but because it wasn't in his nature to stand up any female.

He could do this. It was just one date. Like Aiden said, it wasn't like he was going to marry the woman.

ERIC ARRIVED AT the Espresso Cup the following Thursday morning, ten minutes earlier than his 7:30 a.m. appointment with Evie Bennett, and took a seat where he had a direct line of sight to the entrance while he waited for her.

Yes, he was now privy to her last name, because once he'd gotten home last night after dinner with the guys, he taken a better look at the Boyfriend Experience app, and Evie's profile in particular, to see what information he could glean about her.

Not much, he'd quickly realized. Her last name . . . and that was about it, other than her photo. Considering she was doing the hiring, he supposed it wasn't necessary that she write a bio . . . like the laughable one Dylan had posted for him. He was seriously surprised she'd contacted him after reading the ridiculous, over-the-top paragraph.

If the picture she'd posted was anything to go by, she was very pretty and gave off a girl-next-door kind of vibe. Sweet, unassuming, and the complete opposite of the sophisticated, ambitious, more worldly women he tended to date. Which he chose purposely, because they tended to not be looking for anything more than a good time in bed, and neither was he.

Despite all his objections the previous evening, he was now admittedly intrigued by Evie Bennett, along with the reason she needed to hire a fake boyfriend.

She walked through the doors at 7:29 a.m., and he liked that she was conscientious enough to be on time. Before she spotted him, he did a quick inventory of her appearance. Definitely pretty, with beautiful, shiny brown hair that fell over her shoulders in soft waves. And Jesus Christ, she had the kind of generous hourglass figure a man could lose himself in for hours. The breasts beneath her purple blouse were round and full, and a pair of black skinny jeans outlined her lush hips and accentuated a great pair of legs. He couldn't wait for her to turn around so he could check out her ass.

Yeah, he definitely liked what he saw.

Shifting on her feet, she glanced around the coffee shop, which was fairly busy with people grabbing a cup of designer java before heading off to work for the day. She bit her bottom lip anxiously, and when he finally stood up, she looked in his direction. As soon as they locked gazes, recognition lit up her face.

He made his way toward her, watching her check *him* out this time . . . her light blue eyes taking in his facial features, then a quick sweep of his normal office attire—a short-sleeved, collared shirt and a casual pair of khaki pants.

He watched the rise and fall of her breasts as she inhaled and exhaled a deep breath, as if gathering her fortitude before he reached her. The smile she offered him was tentative, and he returned it with a genuine one of his own meant to put her at ease. When he finally stood in front of her, he held out his hand in greeting.

"Evie Bennett, I presume?" he asked.

"Yes." She slipped her hand into his, her skin soft and warm to the touch, though her grip was impressively firm. "And you're Eric Miller?"

"I am," he replied with a nod of his head. "It's nice to meet you." And shockingly, he meant it.

A light sweep of pink colored her cheeks. "Same."

He nodded toward the counter. "Let's order something to drink before we discuss business. I could use a dose of caffeine. How about you?"

She laughed lightly, relaxing a bit more. "Definitely."

They joined the short line in front of the register, and he glanced from the billboard listing all the fancy beverages to Evie. "What would you like?"

"I'll just take a regular cup of coffee."

"Come on, you can do better than that," he teased. "You don't strike me as being that boring."

She raised a brow, a glimmer of amusement dancing in her eyes. "You've come to that conclusion in the two minutes since meeting me?"

"Am I wrong?" he challenged lightheartedly.

"No," she admitted, a smile tugging at the corner of her very kissable mouth. "I just don't treat myself to a fancy cup of coffee very often. Normally, I'm too rushed in the morning to indulge myself."

They took another step forward in line. "Lucky for you, it's my treat and I *insist* you indulge."

She tipped her head, drawing his gaze to the soft tumble of hair falling over her shoulder and how the ends curled right at the upper swell of her breasts. "Shouldn't I be paying for this, considering the circumstances?"

"Absolutely not," he replied adamantly, forcibly keeping his gaze on her face instead of her chest. "What boyfriend worth his salt would let his girl pay?"

"I haven't hired you *yet*," she reminded him cheekily.

He grinned. He wasn't expecting Evie Bennett to be so impudent, and *surprise, surprise*, he was definitely enjoying their banter, and *her*. "True. Which means I really need to step up my game and impress you."

And honestly, when was the last time he'd *wanted* to make such an effort with the opposite sex? The answer to that eluded him, because truthfully, he couldn't remember being so fascinated and attracted to a woman beyond her physical features. Yet there was no denying that Evie's feisty disposition drew him in and made him want to learn more about her. Which he needed to do anyway if she was going to hire him. And make no mistake, they weren't parting ways until he'd sealed the deal, because she was in the market for a temporary boyfriend, and now that he'd met her, like his campy bio had promised, *he aimed to please.*

"What can I get for the two of you?" the barista asked, pulling Eric's thoughts and attention to the girl waiting for their order.

He glanced at Evie. "Don't disappoint me," he said humorously, referencing the boring cup of coffee she'd mentioned.

A cute, daring smile flitted across her mouth before she looked back at the barista. "I'll take a white chocolate mocha with an extra shot of espresso and whipped cream."

Damn. Was it crazy that he was totally turned on by the fact that she hadn't ordered one of those ridiculous skinny, nonfat, sugar-free lattes that made a mockery of a designer coffee? This was not a girl who'd opt for a salad if she was offered a burger or pizza, and thank God for that. His attraction to her just increased tenfold.

"I'll have an Americano," he said, and handed the girl his credit card.

Once they gave the barista their names for the drinks, they found a small, round vacant table and sat across from each other. He took another sincere look at her pretty features, and combined with her witty, engaging personality he wondered why some guy hadn't already taken her off the market.

Then again, who was he to judge, when he'd made being single and avoiding anything more committed than sex an artform for his entire adult life?

Still, he was curious enough to ask. "So, the million-dollar question. Why would a beautiful woman like you need to hire a fake boyfriend?"

She exhaled a deep breath, prepared to enlighten him just as the barista called out their names for their drink orders. Before she could speak, he held up a finger to stop her.

"Hang on to that thought," he said with a wink as he stood up. "I'll be right back to hear your answer."

CHAPTER THREE

EVIE WATCHED AS Eric walked to the counter to retrieve their order, his stride confident enough to turn a few female heads, not that she could blame any of them for appreciating such masculine perfection. He was even better-looking than his profile pic, and she was still trying to recover from being on the receiving end of those striking green eyes, that breathtakingly sexy smile, and that flirtatious wink.

She pressed a hand to her stomach in hopes of calming the commotion happening inside. She wasn't supposed to be experiencing butterflies. Being attracted to him was one thing . . . feeling like an infatuated schoolgirl was another considering this wasn't a typical date. It was a meeting to discuss the part she needed him to play—a business transaction and nothing more.

As he headed back toward her with both of their drinks in hand, she regained her composure. By the time he sat down across from her again and she had her first sip of her caffeinated latte, she felt like she could carry on an intelligent conversation with him.

"I have to say, hiring someone to be my boyfriend isn't something I'd normally do," she said, not sure why she thought she had to justify her actions to him, but doing it anyway. Maybe because the scenario seemed so . . . desperate, and that's the last thing she wanted him to think. Even if it was partially true.

His eyes twinkled at her from above the rim of his cup as he took a drink of his own coffee before replying. "And offering my services to impersonate a woman's boyfriend isn't something I'd normally do, either."

She laughed at that. "You're the one who signed up to be on the Boyfriend Experience app."

The corner of his mouth quirked with humor. "Touché," he said, as if there was more to his story than met the eye, but he didn't share anything more.

Whatever his reasons for being on the app, she wasn't about to judge. She figured he needed the money, or maybe he just enjoyed randomly dating women and playing the part of a doting boyfriend. Clearly there was a demand for that kind of service, and someone had to fulfill the requests.

"So, back to my question," he said, leaning back casually in his seat, causing his shirt to tighten across his chest, just enough to hint at the toned body beneath. "Why would a beautiful woman like you need to hire a fake boyfriend?"

Her cheeks warmed at his flattery. He definitely had the charm part of his persona down pat, along with a sense of humor. He'd already proven to be kind and considerate by insisting to buy her drink, and overall, he was easy to be with. Maybe because this wasn't a *real* date. She didn't have to impress him since she'd be paying him to do a job, and there were no expectations between them other than what she required from him.

"To make a long story short, my ex cheated on me after four months together," she said, getting the humiliating part of the story out of the way. "He was supposed to attend a family reunion with me over the Fourth of July weekend and meet my parents and relatives for the first time."

Confusion furrowed his brows. "In four

months together, they've never seen a picture of this guy?" he asked incredulously. "Or do I look like him?"

"Ahhh, no, to both questions," she said, and explained. "He's a social worker and doesn't have any social media accounts, and I never sent a picture of him to my parents. But you do share the same first name. I figured you both being an Eric would make me less likely to mess up your name in front of my family."

"Is that why you chose me?" he asked curiously, his gaze holding hers, warm and too damn tempting. "Because our names are the same?"

"Initially, that's what made me click on your profile." She didn't mention that his gorgeous face had been part of what had influenced her decision because that seemed so superficial. "Then I read your bio, and it was quirky and funny and made me laugh, and trust me when I say I need a guy who doesn't take things too seriously, because my parents are a little over-the-top and you're going to need to roll with the punches when it comes to them." And to also deal with her disingenuous, two-faced cousin and her underhanded remarks.

"Can't wait to hear more about them," he

said, grinning as he took another drink of his Americano, giving her a moment to appreciate his long fingers and neatly trimmed nails. "So, are you trying to please your parents by bringing a boyfriend to the reunion? Are they the type who are anxious for you to settle down so they can have grandbabies and you don't want to deal with the whole *when are you getting married* spiel?"

She laughed and shook her head. "No, they've honestly never pressured me."

Turning more serious, Evie absently rubbed her palms along her thighs beneath the table, knowing she needed to clue him in to why she was hiring him so he'd be on his game while interacting with her family, but hating the embarrassing reality of the situation. "The truth is, I don't want to show up at the reunion and have to explain to everyone that I'm no longer with Eric . . . the *other* Eric. They'll want to know what happened, and I'll have to explain the degrading story of being duped and cheated on, and everyone is going to feel sorry for me the entire time I'm there and treat me with kid gloves because they'll think I'm depressed over the breakup."

"Are you? Depressed over how things ended?" he asked.

She shook her head, and since he seemed genuinely interested in her answer, she replied candidly. "No. I'm more angry that I didn't see it coming, and that I dismissed red flags I should have paid more attention to because I didn't want to be one of those paranoid girlfriends who didn't trust their boyfriend. In hindsight, I should have listened to my gut, and now I find it a little hard to trust my own judgment when it comes to . . ." Realizing the direction the conversation was heading, she abruptly stopped talking. The last thing she wanted to do was bare her insecurities to a guy she'd just met or have him feel sorry for her.

"When it comes to men?" He finished the sentence anyway. His low voice, threaded with understanding, prompted her to be honest.

"Yeah." She nodded. "That's why a pretend boyfriend works for me. I'll get through the reunion without being the focus of everyone's attention and I won't look like that pathetic girl who can't keep a guy." Ugh, she was revealing way too much again. "Anyway, by hiring you, I know exactly what to expect, without the complications of an actual boyfriend. We'll play the happy couple for a few days, and when we get back, the transaction is done and we can go our separate ways."

"A few days?" His brows rose in surprise. "So, this is more than a one-day gig?"

She absently bit her bottom lip. "Yes, it's over the Fourth of July holiday weekend next week. Leaving on Friday and returning on Monday. I'm more than willing to pay whatever your fee is, along with all your travel expenses."

It was probably going to cost her a small fortune, but now that she'd spilled her guts to Eric about her situation, she really didn't want to go through the interview process again. And she really did like him. He was easy to be around, and there was no awkward tension between them that relatives would notice or question. The fact that there seemed to be a mutual attraction was a nice bonus, even if it was all a very believable act on his part.

"I'll need to make sure it doesn't interfere with my day job, which I don't think it will since it's a holiday weekend." He finished his coffee and set his paper cup on the table, his gaze meeting hers. "So, tell me what kind of family reunion this is and where we're going for four days."

"It's the immediate family on my father's

side. Most of those relatives live in and around Fresno and Bakersfield, and ever since I was a little girl, every three years, we'd all meet up at a camping resort in Santa Barbara, which is about a four-hour drive away for us here in San Diego."

His seductive mouth curled in an amused grin. "We're going camping? Like with tents and roughing it in the great outdoors?"

"Oh, hell no." She laughed at the thought, even though he didn't seem opposed to the idea. "Did you not hear the 'resort' part of my comment? Everyone has their own small basic cabin to stay in. Just a bed, bathroom, and kitchenette. It's rustic, but there's hot and cold running water and the toilet flushes."

"Thank God for that," he teased.

"My sentiments exactly," she replied seriously. It wasn't glamping, but close enough. "My mother already booked a single, double-sized bed cabin for me and my ex. Unlike most parents, mine are very open-minded when it comes to relationships and . . . well, sleeping arrangements with a boyfriend." Open-minded was an understatement, but Evie wasn't about to scare Eric away with their "free love" mentality, which was just the tip of the iceberg of how unconventional they really were. "I hope you don't have a problem with those arrangements?"

"We'll make it work in a way you're comfortable with," he assured her, and she believed him. So far, he'd been the epitome of a gentleman.

"Okay, then I guess that's it for now, until I hear back from you to confirm your availability next weekend." She glanced at the time on her phone, startled to see so much time had passed, and so quickly. "Oh, wow, I need to get to work. I have a nine o'clock appointment."

Eric nodded. "I need to get to the office, as well."

They both stood up, and he tossed their empty cups in the trash, then held the glass door open for her to walk through before following her out of the Espresso Cup, where they were greeted by the gorgeous, sunny, San Diego summer weather. He lightly pressed a palm to the small of her back, being courteous and respectful, yet her body felt as though it had just been shocked with a high-voltage wire.

Surprised by that startling response, she couldn't stop the tiny, sharp breath she inhaled between her parted lips, and hoped that he hadn't noticed that reflex. Her breasts tingled, her stomach tumbled with awareness, and dear Lord, when was the last time a simple touch from a man had elicited such a rush of heat between her thighs? How about never?

"So, what do you do for work?" he asked, interrupting her body's crazy reaction to him as they headed toward the parking lot and their respective cars.

She forced her mind on answering the question. "I'm a hairstylist. I'm part owner in the Beauty and Bliss Salon and Spa in Hillcrest." She glanced at him, admiring the way the early-morning sun glinted off his hair and outlined his striking profile. "What about you? What do you do for your day job?"

"For you, I'm a social worker," he replied with one of those slow, knee-weakening winks that made her toes curl and her nipples peak. "But in my real life, I work at Prestige Car Services."

"Oh, like a mechanic?" Surprising, since she hadn't seen any grease under his nails.

He chuckled and shook his head. "No, not that kind of car service. Prestige Car Services is a company that caters to clients who need a personal driver, for whatever reason."

"So you're a chauffeur?"

Another flicker of humor brightened his green eyes, the outer layers of gold more prominent in the sun. "Yeah, something like that," he replied, his ambiguous tone making her wonder what he was hiding. Not that it mattered, as long as whatever he did for his day job didn't affect his boyfriend duties.

They came to her vehicle, an older compact model that was basic and no-frills. She could have afforded something current, but she couldn't justify a four-hundred-dollar-a-month car payment when this one was completely paid off. It wasn't shiny and new, but it got her where she needed to go and gave her great gas mileage. Now that the salon was finally bringing in a nice profit for all three of them, Evie was saving that extra money for a down payment to buy her own condo someday—especially now that she was going to be single for the foreseeable future.

"I'll need your phone number so I can contact you," he said, taking his iPhone out of his front pocket just as she unlocked the driver's-side door.

"Oh, of course." She'd assumed they'd communicate through the app, but had no problem giving him access to contact her more directly.

She gave him her digits, which he typed into his phone. When he finally finished inputting her information, her own phone, which was in her purse, chimed with a message notification.

He glanced up at her and grinned. "That was me. I just texted you, so now you have my phone number, as well."

With that, he opened the car door for her and she slid inside. He braced a forearm against the doorframe and leaned in closer, filling the inside of her vehicle with the enticing scent of his cologne. God, he smelled ridiculously good, and once again her body responded to the warm, woodsy fragrance that was as arousing as the man himself. It was all she could do to keep from squirming in her seat as she met his unapologetically direct gaze that was focused on her mouth. Which in turn caused her to nervously lick her bottom lip.

His slow, satisfied smile felt like a physical caress and clearly solidified that there was nothing pretend or fake about the simmering chemistry between them. It was a complication she really didn't need, but then again, it would definitely add to the realistic appearance of a relationship if he was able to accompany her to Santa Barbara next weekend.

"I'll be in touch, Evie Bennett," he said, his voice deep and husky.

He stepped back and closed her door, and she watched in her rearview mirror as he walked to the row of cars behind hers and got into a dark gray sporty BMW. Wow . . . all she could think was that he must have been a damn good chauffeur who made a lucrative amount in tips to afford a luxury car like that.

He drove off and she started her own car, then reached into her purse to check her phone for any missed calls or messages before she headed to work. There was only one text message . . . the one that Eric had sent to her so she'd have his phone number, too.

She clicked on the notification to read what he'd written. *Just so you know, I think you have a great ass.*

Her jaw dropped in shock, but not because she was offended. The message was so unexpected . . . and dammit, so satisfying and flattering, when she'd been feeling so insecure about herself after what had happened with the *other* Eric. She liked knowing that another guy appreciated her curves. Especially *this* guy.

Thank you, she typed back, and hesitated only a few beats before brazenly adding, *Just for the record, so do you.* She wasn't going to lie . . . she'd noticed his firm butt when he'd walked up to the counter to grab their drinks.

She imagined him chuckling as those dancing bubbles appeared on her screen as he formed his response. It came a few seconds later. *Ms. Bennett, I think you and I are going to get along just fine.*

The winky face emoticon he added at the end of the sentence put those butterflies right back into her stomach again.

As pretend boyfriend material, the man was good. *Really* good.

ERIC WALKED INTO the office with a cheerful smile on his face that Heather, the receptionist at Prestige Car Services, noticed immediately and didn't hesitate to point out.

She arched a brow at Eric as she reached for a few pink message slips and handed them to him. "Someone must have had a good morning . . . or a good night that lasted *through* to the morning," she added meaningfully.

It was no secret to anyone, especially the people in his office and the drivers he and Leo employed, that he was a player, so to speak. While he didn't do long-term relationships, he was a twenty-nine-year-old man with a healthy sex drive, and yeah, that meant having occasional sleepovers with women.

Rolling his eyes at her comment, Eric glanced through the calls he'd already missed that morning, while prioritizing the messages by importance.

Today, however, his upbeat disposition had nothing to do with waking up to a woman's mouth wrapped around his dick and instead was a direct result of his highly enjoyable meeting with Evie Bennett, where the only physical contact he'd had with her was when he'd deliberately placed his hand on her lower back.

There had been nothing overtly sexual about the gesture, but he'd heard her tiny gasp of awareness, and damn if her satisfying reaction didn't make him want to brazenly caress his palm a bit lower, over the ample curve of the ass he'd noticed back at the coffee shop, just to see if it felt as sweet in his hand as it looked encased in her formfitting jeans.

Somehow, he'd managed to resist that particular temptation but hadn't hesitated to text her exactly what he thought of her luscious backside for her to read after he drove away. It had been bold and risky, certainly, but when she'd typed back her own cheeky response that made him laugh out loud, he'd known right then and there that this funny, endearing woman who'd been recently burned by a cheating asshole of an ex was one he wanted to spend the Fourth of July weekend with . . . because he genuinely liked her. A lot.

Go figure, he mused, feeling another grin tug at his lips. Even he was surprised that thoughts of her had lingered on the short drive to the office, when he'd always been so good at compartmentalizing his time with women and not allowing them to consume his thoughts once they parted ways. It was safer that way and assured messy emotions didn't get involved, and up until this point, putting that barrier between himself and his dates had been incredibly easy to do . . . much to *their* frustration.

But Evie Bennett was . . . different. Maybe it was the fact that she was the polar opposite of all those other women he tended to gravitate toward that intrigued him. In the short time they'd been at the Espresso Cup, she'd amused him, impressed him, aroused him . . . but it had been those few times he'd glimpsed moments of vulnerability when she'd talked about her ex that stirred something deeper inside him. Something oddly protective, along with the unfamiliar need to show her that she deserved so much better than a douchebag who didn't appreciate the woman she was.

"Oh my God," Heather said, the gleeful tone of her voice pulling Eric from his thoughts. "You *totally* got laid this morning, didn't you? That smile you walked in with hasn't left your face, and I've never seen you so distracted. You've been staring at the same message for the past five minutes."

"Get your mind out of the gutter," he said, unwilling to give up any of the truth, especially that a woman he'd *just met* was responsible for his perma-grin. "Not that it's any of your business, but I'll have you know I spent the night alone, and it is possible for me to be in a good mood in the morning just because it's a great morning. And I was distracted because I was thinking of how I need to respond to Bob Aguilar's message before I call him back."

"Hmmm," she hummed, clearly not believing him. "If you say so."

The phone on Heather's desk rang, and as she picked up the receiver and greeted the person on the other line, Eric took advantage of the interruption and headed down the short hallway to Leo's office. He knew his friend and business partner was already in, since Eric had parked next to Leo's car.

As soon as he walked inside, the other man glanced up from the laptop open on his desk and stopped typing. "Happy to escape the third degree out there?" he asked, laughing.

"Jesus Christ, yes," Eric muttered in a low voice while closing the door, because he didn't need Heather overhearing his conversation about Evie with Leo.

"So, how did it go?" Leo asked as soon as Eric was settled in one of the chairs in front of his friend's desk. "Did you completely crush the girl's hopes?"

Eric realized he could have gently and politely turned down Evie at any point during their meeting this morning. Hell, he could have admitted the truth, that he'd been added to the app as a joke and wasn't interested in being anyone's fake boyfriend and he was sorry for taking up her time . . . but he hadn't. Even when the opportunity had openly presented itself and she'd blithely pointed out that he'd signed up to be on the Boyfriend Experience app *after* he'd told her that he didn't normally offer his services to impersonate a woman's significant other, he'd still played it off.

"I still think Dylan is a royal jerk for doing what he did. However, after meeting Evie, I really like her," he admitted with what he hoped was a casual shrug. "She was very sweet and I don't want to hurt her feelings when it's easy enough for me to help her out."

Okay, that was a blatant lie. Hurting her feelings had nothing to do with the reasons he was going to accompany Evie to her family reunion, but Leo didn't need to know that. His decision was a bit more selfish. She needed a temporary boyfriend and, well, Eric wanted the chance to kiss those full, sensual lips . . . and maybe even run his fingers through her soft, beautiful hair while palming her delectable ass—which, in his opinion, would add to the whole boyfriend experience, right? Better than turning her down and letting some other jackass be her boyfriend for the weekend. His hands clenched at his sides at the very thought.

Leo leaned back in his chair and smirked. "Wow, look at you, being so charitable, especially since sweet is so not your type. But at least that way you'll be able to keep your dick in your pants."

Apparently sweet *was* his type, when it was wrapped up in a curvy package like Evie's body, because his dick had definitely noticed and appreciated her voluptuous figure. Combine that with her irrepressible personality, and he was fairly certain he was going to enjoy his temporary time with her.

"So, what does she need to hire a boyfriend for?" Leo asked curiously.

"A family reunion over the Fourth of July weekend. She recently broke up with a boyfriend she was going to take to meet her parents. The guy cheated on her, and she doesn't want to have to deal with explaining the situation to relatives or be the center of everyone's sympathy, though I'm sure she'll tell her parents about the split at some point after she gets back home."

"So she's going to be calling you by some other guy's name all weekend?" Leo shook his head. "At least with Peyton, she used my real name when she fabricated our relationship to her parents, so there wasn't any confusion."

"The guy's name that she was dating was

also Eric, so no chance of mixing up names."

"See, it's kismet," Leo said with exaggerated humor. "The two of you were meant to be."

"Don't be a dumb ass," Eric said, laughing. "This is not fate or destiny or any other romanticized version of meeting my soul mate. I'm just doing Evie a favor because I've got three dares from you, Dylan, and Aiden sitting on my head," he reminded his friend, though truthfully, that challenge hadn't played a part in his decision at all. "And honestly, she's a nice girl who doesn't want to deal with family drama for a weekend, and I can help provide that diversion, so why not have some fun with the situation?"

"Yeah, why not?" Leo said, nodding his head in agreement. "How long is this family reunion thing, anyway?"

"It's next Friday through Monday. I wanted to make sure there's nothing booked that you'll need me for over that weekend before I confirm with Evie?" Even though they were equal partners in the business, Eric always liked to clear his personal days off with Leo, and vice versa.

"Not that I can think of, but let me double-check." Leaning forward, Leo pulled up their schedule on his computer that listed their drivers, the fleet of cars they owned, and what was scheduled on each day. "Looks like it's a pretty straightforward weekend since it's a long holiday."

"Perfect." He stood up, needing to return a few of the calls he'd received while he'd been with Evie. "Of course, I'll have my cell phone on me, and it's only in Santa Barbara, so in an emergency, I could be back in four hours."

"Just go and forget about work, okay?" Leo said, his tone serious. "You hardly ever take any time off. And that's what we hired fleet managers for, to keep things organized and scheduled so we can have more free time to ourselves."

There had been a time when he and Leo had been the only two drivers in their company, and it was still hard to believe how much they'd grown and how far they'd come. "Okay," he agreed, because he knew if Leo really needed him, he'd pick up the phone and call.

He headed across the hall to his office and started his day returning phone calls. He spent a few hours making changes to a contract with their attorney that a new client wanted them to sign that included an NDA, which wasn't an issue, but Eric wanted to make sure their ass was covered. He and Leo had lunch with business investors to discuss their plans to open other offices in different states and major cities, and the afternoon was spent signing off on maintenance inspections they'd scheduled on a few of their vehicles.

If the day wasn't busy enough, at six p.m., he and Leo met with another wealthy client who was in town for dinner. What should have been an hour-and-a-half-max meal turned into nearly three hours of business conversation that ended with a few new promising leads both he and Leo planned to pursue over the next couple of weeks.

By the time Eric arrived home later that evening, it was almost ten and he was exhausted. The first thing he did was take a long, hot shower. The steam loosened the tension across his shoulders, and the half-dozen body jets pummeled and massaged his muscles until he felt relaxed and his mind had wound down from his packed schedule.

He hadn't had five extra minutes to himself all day to contact Evie to let her know he was definitely free the following weekend to accompany her to her family reunion. As he settled into bed, he thought about dialing her number right now, but nixed the idea for two reasons.

One, it was late and he didn't want to wake her if she was out for the night, although he wouldn't have minded listening to the sleep-husky sound of her voice in his ear, he thought as he absently stroked a hand down his bare torso.

And two, he'd rather deliver the news face-to-face, because quite frankly, even though contacting her by phone or text messaging was the simplest, easiest, cut-and-dried route, he couldn't deny the most important reason for not calling her tonight . . . because he wanted an excuse to see Evie in person again.

CHAPTER FOUR

E VIE STOOD IN front of her designated cupboard in the storeroom of Beauty and Bliss, trying to focus on updating her weekly inventory list of hair products—mainly to keep her mind off of the fact that she hadn't heard back from Eric. Granted, it had only been twenty-four hours since she'd propositioned him at the Espresso Cup, but she'd thought, or rather hoped, that she would have heard his answer by the end of the day. Instead, she'd heard nothing but crickets.

Yesterday, she'd obsessively checked her phone between clients and after work, right up to the point that she finally forced herself to silence the device and get some sleep. But, pathetically, the first thing she'd done when she'd woken up was check for any messages . . . only to find none.

So, her day had started with a nice dose of disappointment, along with the realization that she might have only imagined the attraction between them. It was certainly a possibility that she'd read more into the way he'd looked at her, or even his flirty text about her ass. It was even a bigger likelihood that she'd misjudged the entire situation, considering how she'd completely let her most recent ex pull the wool over her eyes for four months. Hell, he obviously didn't even want to be her *fake* boyfriend.

When had she become so naive when it came to trusting men? she thought in frustration. Oh, yeah, that first lesson had been taught by Graham, who'd broken up with her and was now engaged to Evie's cousin, Raquel. It had taken Evie a long time to let her guard down with a man again, and what did she get for her efforts? Another huge kick in the heart courtesy of Eric number one.

Eric number two hadn't seemed like a guy who'd blow her off, especially since he was on an app to service women and build a side business, and as a beta tester, she was encouraged to rate her experience with him. A review stating that he "leaves a woman hanging" wouldn't be great for his reputation, but that's how she was beginning to feel . . . like she'd been stood up. That maybe he hadn't liked what he saw and changed his mind about spending four days with her. *Thank you very much for that, insecurities.*

She shook her head of those thoughts and refocused on her inventory. She only had a half hour before her next client arrived for highlights, and she needed to get her supplies ordered so she didn't run out before Monday, which was the last Monday of the month and a day she, Scarlett, and Jessica opened the shop exclusively for the Beautiful You program Evie had created a year ago as a way to give back to the community.

Normally, every Sunday and Monday the shop was closed, with the exception of the once-a-month Beautiful You day, when women from the local domestic assault shelters came in for a free haircut, manicure, or facial at no charge to them. Evie saw it as a fun day of pampering, building self-confidence, and empowering those less fortunate women to embrace their beauty, inside and out. It was also a long, extremely exhausting day, with appointments booked back to back, but witnessing each woman's transformation and being the recipient of their gratitude and radiant smiles as they walked out of the salon was the best feeling ever.

Fifteen minutes later, just as Evie finished her online purchase of inventory and was walking out of the storeroom, she nearly collided with Scarlett in the hallway, who had a gleeful look on her face.

"Oh my God, Evie," she said in a hushed whisper that was threaded with excitement. "There is an *insanely* hot guy out at the front desk asking for you. I'm pretty sure it's your fake boyfriend. And if it's not, I call first dibs on him over Jessica."

Evie's stomach flipped at the thought that Eric might be here. Still, she couldn't help but laugh, even knowing Scarlett was completely serious. When Evie had arrived at work yesterday morning after her coffee date with Eric, both of her business partners had grilled her about him, and they'd waited just as anxiously throughout the day for her to hear back from him.

This morning, when she'd walked through the doors and had to confess that he still hadn't contacted her, she'd been treated to those sympathetic looks she hated so much—even though she knew her best friends meant well—along with man-bashing comments meant to make her feel better that had only made the whole situation worse. She'd been glad to have getting her inventory done as a legit reason to escape to the storeroom and their attempts to soothe her bruised female ego.

But clearly, now Scarlett was singing a very different tune about men after laying eyes on a gorgeous guy. Evie didn't want to get her hopes up that it was Eric, because the truth was, it could be a male client who had been referred to her, but she straightened her shoulders and put on a smile as she walked out into the reception area to meet Hot Guy.

Her traitorous heart did a tiny flip-flop in her chest when tall, dark-haired, extremely attractive Eric Miller came into view—definitely hot guy material in every way—and when he saw her approaching, a disarmingly sexy smile formed on his lips as he met her gaze.

"Good morning," he said when she reached him, his low, husky voice pouring over her like warm honey, which in turn made her feel equally gooey inside. "I was in the neighborhood and thought I'd bring you that coffee you never have time to indulge in on your way to work."

He offered her the large paper cup he held

in his hand, imprinted with the name the Espresso Cup. "White chocolate mocha with an extra shot of espresso and whipped cream, right?"

She blinked at him, shocked and impressed that he'd remembered such a specific drink order, but he was clearly a guy who didn't miss even the most minute details considering he'd remembered the name of her salon, too.

She accepted the latte with a smile. "Yes, that's correct. Thank you," she said, keenly aware that they were being watched, and very blatantly, by her two partners and their curious clients. "That was very nice of you."

His green eyes twinkled playfully. "It was my pleasure."

God, the way the word *pleasure* rolled off his tongue was so decadent and sinful.

His own gaze did a quick sweep of the shop, which was completely, awkwardly silent, as if everyone was waiting with bated breath to hear what he had to say to her.

Absently, he ran his fingers through his hair, disheveling the strands in a way that only added to his masculine appeal. "Do you mind if we take this conversation outside?"

He was obviously just as mindful of their

avid audience, and she appreciated the suggestion. "Sure."

Setting her drink down on the reception counter, she followed him out the main door to the sidewalk in front of Beauty and Bliss. The shop was framed by huge glass windows, and while their discussion was now private, the two of them were still on display and the women inside were *not* discreet about their staring. She was going to kill her two friends for being so damn nosey.

She crossed her arms over her chest to brace herself for a possible rejection, which was silly because if he was going to say no to her weekend proposition, wouldn't he have just done it by phone?

His gaze dipped, sliding down to the upper swells of her breasts that she'd just inadvertently offered up for his perusal. He didn't linger long, just enough to start a slow burn in the pit of her stomach before his eyes made their way back up to her now flushed face. It took everything in her not to shift restlessly on her feet or melt into a puddle at the approving curve to his lips. Apparently, Eric Miller was not only an ass man but a breast man, as well.

She was desperate to dispel the sexual tension vibrating inside her. "So, what brings you by, other than delivering coffee?" Somehow, she managed to keep her tone even and businesslike.

"First and foremost, I wanted to apologize for not getting in touch with you yesterday," he said, his tone sincere. "I had every intention of calling, but I was slammed at work from the moment I walked into the office. And by the time I got home last night, it was after ten and I didn't want to risk waking you up."

His legitimate reason for ignoring her after their meeting softened Evie's defenses, and her arms and shoulders relaxed a fraction.

"I thought an in-person apology was better than in impersonal text, and I was hoping the coffee would earn me some bonus points for going silent yesterday," he said, offering her a charming smile that was completely unfair because it made her forget everything but how goddamn sexy and attractive he was. And persuasive, too.

"It did," she admitted.

He appeared satisfied to hear his ploy had worked. "I was also curious to see where you worked and what your shop was like. I should know all that information if I'm your boyfriend, right?"

It took a few extra seconds for his insinuation to sink in, but she wasn't going to get too excited until she had a firm confirmation from him. "Does that mean you're available for me to hire for all of next weekend?" She couldn't disguise the hope in her voice.

His low, husky laugh was like a caress across her skin. "Yes, that's exactly what it means, Evie Bennett."

"Oh my God. Thank you!" A huge wave of relief washed over her, and she reacted without thinking, closing the short distance between them and wrapping her arms around his neck to hug him in gratitude.

As soon as she was pressed tight against him, with her softer feminine curves aligned to his harder masculine body and her cheek rubbing along his slightly rougher skin, that initial gesture of appreciation veered in a whole different direction as awareness slammed her senses. A hard, muscular body she shamelessly wanted to feel naked against hers and warm skin scented with an arousing combination of cologne and pure man that tempted her to bury her face against his neck and breathe deeply of that intoxicating fragrance.

He groaned into her ear, the sound tortured, and his hands gripped her waist, though not to push her away but to draw her closer. "You do realize, don't you, that we have four women in your shop staring at us and I'm trying like hell not to do something completely ungentlemanly right now, like slid my hand over your ass and cop a feel?"

His words snapped her out of the sensual fog she'd just lost herself in, and she jumped back from him, embarrassment flooding through her. "Oh my God, I'm so sorry," she said in a rush, her eyes wide and her cheeks warming with chagrin. "That was incredibly inappropriate. I mean, I shouldn't have—"

"Evie," he said, his voice a bit gruff and desire darkening his green eyes. "Stop apologizing. I'm glad you're comfortable with physical affection. It'll make the whole boyfriend experience much more believable if I can touch you intimately."

Touch her intimately? Her inner bad girl was already on board with the idea of feeling this man's capable hands on her body. She absently licked her bottom lip at the seductive thought.

His gaze narrowed at the spot where her

tongue had just skimmed. "Stop tempting me with your mouth," he ordered on a low, frustrated growl that made her nipples peak.

Confusion swirled through her foggy mind. How was she teasing him when they were standing nearly a foot apart? "What?"

He reached out and rested his hand along her jaw and brushed the pad of his thumb along her damp lower lip, heedless of who might see. "Every time your tongue glides across your bottom lip, which you do often, all I can think about is kissing you long and deep to see if you taste like cotton candy or cinnamon red hots."

She visibly shivered, and a slow, stomach-tumbling smile eased across his face at her telling reaction.

"I'm dying to know," he murmured, boldly pressing his thumb against the pillowed flesh until the tip of his finger grazed her bottom teeth and she tasted the salt on his skin. "But when it happens, and trust me when I say that it *will* happen, I don't want an audience. I want the luxury of taking my time and exploring every inch of your soft, sweet mouth."

She was utterly breathless, because that's how this man made her feel. And those come-hither eyes . . . God, how was she going to survive four days of looking into them without falling headlong into all sorts of trouble?

"Hey," he asked, letting his hand fall away, much to her disappointment. "You okay?"

She gave her head a small shake to snap herself out of her stupor. "Umm, yeah. You've very convincing."

He arched a dark, challenging brow. "It wasn't an act, sweetheart. Don't make me prove it in front of your friends and everyone else driving by, or that woman entering your shop right now who's staring at us, too."

She glanced over her shoulder to see who he was referring to and recognized her client. "That's my nine o'clock appointment so I need to go."

He nodded in understanding. "I'm going to be busy this weekend, but I'll be in touch when I can so we can discuss everything the boyfriend experience entails," he told her with a wink as he took his car keys from his front pocket. "And don't hesitate to text me if you have any questions."

"Okay."

He gave her his signature sexy grin, along with a wave, and she couldn't help but watch him head toward his car, just long enough to admire his perfect backside before she went inside the shop. She was immediately greeted with clapping and enthusiastic woo-hoos and all the girls talking at once.

"Holy smokes, can a guy get any hotter?"

"Oh my God, we thought he was going to kiss you!"

"Is that sexy piece of man candy really yours for four whole days?"

"Everyone, *stop*," Evie insisted, pressing her hands to her flaming cheeks, though she was smiling because who wouldn't be after such a wildly flirtatious encounter with a man who was sex on two legs?

Jessica gave Evie a once-over that was direct and playful. "You, Ms. Evie Bennett, are a smitten kitten."

Evie laughed and thought about denying it, but Jessica would just relentlessly persist until she admitted the truth. "Maybe. Just a little," she conceded, allowing herself to enjoy the infatuated feeling, only because she knew there was nothing real about the relationship. It was all just physical attraction and fun playacting, and she was okay with that. "I'm only a smitten kitten because he's really good at his job and providing the whole boyfriend experience."

"Okay, if that's what you want to tell yourself," Scarlett added in a droll tone. "But from our perspective, he didn't look like he was faking *anything*."

She shook her head and rolled her eyes, ready to move on from all the attention focused on her. "Your entertainment for the morning is over and I need to get to work." Evie waved away all the women but her client, Marcy, who she led to her station with her coffee in her hand to enjoy while Marcy's highlights were processing.

As Evie started her day, she realized that there was one thing that she and Eric hadn't settled on yet . . . what his fee would be for his time and service for four days. She knew he probably wasn't cheap, but he was definitely worth whatever price he charged because he was *that* good.

CHAPTER FIVE

J UST LIKE EVERY other Sunday at four o'clock in the afternoon, Eric parked his car in the driveway of the small three-bedroom childhood home where he'd grown up and where his mother now lived by herself as a part of the divorce settlement she'd received from Eric's father almost ten years ago.

On the passenger seat next to him were two bags of groceries and a bouquet of flowers that he'd picked up at the market. Same routine, different weekend, not that his mother ever noticed his efforts. Or if Ginny Miller did recognize his attempts to bring some normalcy to their lives, she didn't mention it or thank him for the meal he cooked or make him feel like he had a place in the house anymore since it was now filled with an overbearing sadness and bittersweet memories he couldn't compete with.

At this point in his life, he'd accepted that his mother's aloof manner would probably never change, and even knowing that painful truth, he also knew it wouldn't stop him from visiting her. Despite the huge disconnect between them, he was still her son, she was still his mother, and he refused to cut her off emotionally the way she had him when his twin sister, Trisha, had died at the age of sixteen.

He exhaled what felt like a weary, soul-deep sigh as his gaze took in the front of the house, remembering much happier times when the Millers had been the equivalent of a picture-perfect Rockwell family. His parents hadn't been rich, but they'd been loving and focused on making their kids' lives their priority.

Up until he and Trisha had turned fifteen, the four of them had spent idyllic summer vacations at the beach together. Even with Trisha in soccer and Eric in football, their parents had always found a way to attend their sporting events and cheer them on. Eric had spent endless hours with his father in the garage, tinkering with car parts and learning how to rebuild an engine, while his sister and mom spent the weekends out in the backyard, tending to the roses and garden they'd nurtured together.

Despite normal squabbles with his sister

heading into their teen years, as twins they'd been best friends. All his life, Trisha had been his person, his other half of that twin connection they'd shared from birth, and when she'd died as he held her hand, he knew he'd never be the same again. Sitting at her bedside, with Trisha's thin, weary body finally succumbing to the awful leukemia that ravaged her for the past year, he'd felt his heart being ripped painfully from his chest during those last few gasps. She'd taken a huge piece of him with her when she'd drawn her last breath, leaving an eternal void he felt even now.

His heart had shattered that day, in a way he never wanted to experience ever again. With Trisha gone, he'd felt so lost and alone and empty inside, with no one to turn to for comfort because his parents had been wrapped up in their own grief and anger over the loss of their daughter, leaving Eric to blindly find his own way through the pain and sorrow eating him up inside.

A house that had once been filled with love, laughter, and happiness had been cast with a pallor of sadness and despair. Once Trisha had been buried, his parents stopped talking and touching and spent more time apart than together. His dad deliberately worked long hours, and his mother had withdrawn into a deep, dark depression where she slept for days, and when she was awake for any length of time, she operated on autopilot.

And Eric . . . well, he'd realized that he'd not only lost his best friend and twin sister, but he'd lost his entire family all in one fell swoop.

The two years following Trisha's death had been excruciating, mentally and emotionally, and it had been a huge relief to Eric when his estranged parents finally divorced and he'd moved into a dorm at San Diego State University. Being out of the bleak and oppressive situation on a daily basis, he'd finally been able to breathe and make some kind of new normal for himself.

But there was no denying how much he missed Trisha and how badly her death had affected him and still did. Survivor's guilt had plagued him for years, and even though a part of him had come to peace with the situation, there were still triggers that brought back the heartache and pain of losing her. The birthday they'd once shared and the date of her death were still his hardest days to get through.

But today was about spending time with his

mother, Eric reminded himself. Grabbing the two plastic-handled grocery bags and the cellophane-wrapped flowers, he got out of the car and started up the walkway to the front of the house. Halfway there, a monarch butterfly fluttered around his head, and he smiled, feeling his sister's presence near him.

He wasn't one to normally believe in the supernatural, but his sister had been obsessed with butterflies growing up, and they'd been naturally drawn to Trisha, trusting her enough to land on her shoulder or her hand. Eric had always been envious because they'd always given him a wide berth, probably because he hadn't been as gentle as his sister, but a few weeks after she'd passed, he'd been in the front yard when a monarch started annoying the crap out of him . . . flying in front of his face, landing on his head, and ignoring his attempts to shoo the pesky insect away.

In a moment of weird clarity, he'd known this was his sister's way of visiting him, to let him know that she was okay and watching over him . . . not that he'd ever told anyone about his occasional encounter with those monarch butterflies. But their presence always calmed and reassured him in a way he couldn't explain.

"I miss you, Trish," he whispered, and with that, the butterfly swirled one more time around his head before flying away.

He continued to the front porch, and knowing the door would be locked, as it always was, and his mother was probably in the backyard, like she always was, he tucked the flowers under one arm so he could use his key to let himself inside. Everything was predictably quiet as he closed the door, the drawn drapes in the living room making the house much too dark and somber. But that, too, was normal.

As he headed into the kitchen, he passed by the long, decorative table his mother had set up as a memorial for Trish after she'd died. A crystal cut vase held beautiful white roses that he knew his mother replaced every single day and at least a dozen framed photographs of his sister, from infant stage all the way to age fifteen lined the table . . . the last picture having been taken right before her cancer diagnosis, when she still looked healthy and happy.

With that abrupt end to the framed photos, it was always a reminder to Eric of a life cut too short. Just like the last time he'd dared to look into his sister's bedroom years ago and found it the same exact way it had been the day she'd been taken to the hospital for the last time. Untouched. Preserved. It still looked like the room of a sixteen-year-old girl.

Unlike Eric's bedroom, which his mother had turned into a reading room for herself, with all traces of his childhood gone.

In the kitchen, he set the bags and flowers on the counter, and a glance out the window above the sink confirmed that his mother was, in fact, out back, tending to the same garden and white roses that she and Trish had planted together so long ago.

He didn't bother telling his mother he was there. She knew what time he always arrived on Sunday, and she'd eventually make her way inside. Instead, he unloaded the items he'd bought at the market and started making dinner for the two of them, always preparing more than needed so she'd have leftovers for a few days. An hour later, he was pulling baked ziti from the oven when his mother came through the sliding glass door leading into the house from the backyard.

She was in an old, faded T-shirt and a pair of those pants that women wore that ended at her calves. Her hair, which once was a sleek bob and had been a dark russet brown, was now unruly curls with more gray than color. She hadn't made the effort to wear makeup in a very long time, and while he'd always think of his mother as beautiful, he couldn't help but compare this plain version of Ginny Miller to the vibrant woman who used to take pride in her appearance.

"Hi, Mom," he said, walking over to place a kiss on her cheek, which she offered up to him. She smelled like sunshine and dirt . . . when he once remembered her being wrapped in the scent of the chocolate chip cookies she used to make for him and Trish. "How are you doing today?"

"Good," she replied automatically as she washed her hands in the sink and gave him a small smile that was only a fraction of what it had once been, in happier times. "And you?"

He slathered a few slices of French bread with the garlic butter he'd made and set them on a baking sheet. "Same." Yep, same general conversation every Sunday, too.

"Dinner smells good."

He glanced at her and smiled. "I made baked ziti." Every weekend, he chose a child-hood favorite to make for her, always hoping it would bond them somehow, or at least spur his mother to cook again, something she'd loved doing. So far, neither had happened. "While I finish broiling the garlic bread, will you set the table and put your flowers in a vase?"

"Sure."

She did what he requested, while he slid the bread under the broiler to give it a quick bake to crisp the edges. Once that was done, they both made their own plates, she poured them each a glass of iced tea, and they sat down at the table together.

"How was work this past week?" he asked, grateful that her part-time job at a local nursery forced her to get out of the house and be around people. She took care of watering the plants and flowers, keeping them alive and making them look pretty until they were bought. The position was perfect for her.

"It was busy." She pushed her pasta around on her plate before taking a small bite. "I saw Patty Henderson. She came into the nursery to buy some succulents. It's been years since I've seen her."

"Yes, it has been."

Eric stared at his mother's face, trying to figure out how she *really* felt about seeing a woman who'd once been one of her closest, dearest friends, *before* Trish's death, but her expression revealed nothing. Within the first six months of his sister's passing, his mother had closed herself off from everyone, to the point that even her best friends stopped calling and no longer came by the house because she refused to see or talk to them. Instead, she'd wallowed in her pain and grief alone, and those friendships had never recovered from being cut off.

"How is Patty?" he asked, to keep the conversation flowing.

"She looked well." Absently, Ginny picked at her garlic bread, her appetite already gone. "She asked if I'd like to go to lunch sometime."

Eric glanced up from his ziti, feeling a glimmer of hope and trying not to push too hard at this new and positive olive branch Patty had extended. "And what did you say?"

"That...I... ummm, wasn't sure." His mother's eyes met his, and he felt punched in the gut by the loneliness he saw there, along with the desire to reconnect with a friend warring with the fear of getting close to anyone ever again. "After all these years, I'm afraid it would be so awkward."

Initially, he knew it probably would be a little uncomfortable, until someone broke the ice and their old friendship kicked back into gear. "Mom, she wouldn't have asked you to lunch if she genuinely didn't want to see and talk to you outside of the nursery."

Ginny fiddled with her fork. "She gave me her phone number, but I just don't know."

"You should think about it." He reached out and gently squeezed her hand and was surprised when he felt her fingers tighten ever so slightly around his. "Patty was your best friend."

His mother nodded, that sadness still lingering, and Eric wasn't going to push the issue. Any decision his mother made had to be of her own volition.

He finished off his garlic bread and wiped his buttery fingers on his napkin. "So, I wanted to let you know that I won't be by next Sunday with dinner. I'll be out of town for the weekend."

"Where are you going?" she asked, mildly curious.

"To Santa Barbara with a friend to visit her family for the Fourth of July weekend."

A tiny spark of interest lit her eyes. "Her?"

The fact that his mother had jumped on the

pronoun made him smile. "Yes. A woman. Her name is Evie and we're just . . . friends." He wasn't sure how to label their non-relationship, and the whole fake boyfriend situation was too complicated to explain to his mother, who didn't understand much about social media or apps or dating trends these days.

"And you're meeting her family?" she asked, making Eric aware of just how much his mother had paid attention to this particular conversation. "Is it serious?"

Again, he kept things simple. "Yes, I'm meeting her family, and no, it's not serious."

"Oh," she said quietly.

Was she disappointed? He couldn't tell. They'd never discussed his love life, and he'd certainly never brought a woman home to meet his mom. For one thing, no female had ever made him *want* to introduce her to his mother, and secondly, he didn't want his mom reading more into a relationship than the hookup situation it always was. Bottom line, his mother did not need to know about or meet the women he casually slept with.

Eric ate the last bite of ziti on his plate, and recognizing the signs that his mother was finished eating as well, he picked up their dishes and carried them to the sink. They fell into the same old routine . . . he loaded the plates and silverware into the dishwasher, and she put away the leftovers. They finished about the same time, and he turned around to face her while drying off his hands.

"Is there anything you need me to do around here before I go?" he asked like always, because things did occasionally break when it came to a house that was over thirty years old. He did his best to fix whatever he could when it came to keeping up his mother's house, and what he couldn't figure out, he hired someone else to do.

"No, everything is fine," she replied, looking a little distracted.

He wondered if she was thinking about what he'd said about reaching out to Patty. God, he hoped so, but time would tell.

"If you need anything at all, just call me," he said, always meaning it.

He wrapped her in a hug, and she tentatively touched her hands to his back to return the embrace, clinging to him a little closer than normal. She felt especially fragile and vulnerable tonight, as if she'd lost her way over the past thirteen years and didn't know how to find her way back again.

"I'm always here for you, Mom," he told her as they shared an emotional moment that made his throat feel tight. "I love you."

She hugged him a little tighter before letting go and stepping back. "I love you, too, son."

She'd said the words many times to him since Trish's death, usually in response to him saying it first, but this time, as he looked into her eyes, they weren't hazed over with the usual underlying grief and pain and depression. There was the smallest glimmer of the mother he used to know, the one who'd smiled often and loved with her whole heart until her identity as a mother had been shattered, just as his as a brother had been.

He left his mother's, and by the time he reached his own house, it was seven o'clock at night. Still early, and he really didn't want to spend the rest of the evening by himself, rehashing his time with his mother and reading more into her actions than he should, because he'd been disappointed before.

What he needed was a distraction. Something, or someone, to take his thoughts off of his visit with his mother. He had at least a dozen contacts in his phone of willing females who'd be up for a booty call, but honestly, none of those women remotely appealed to him. No, the only person that filled his mind was Evie, who he hadn't spoken to since Friday at her shop because his weekend had been extremely busy.

He decided he needed to rectify that situation. Kicking off his shoes, he made himself comfortable on the couch, called her number on his phone, and waited to hear her voice.

CHAPTER SIX

E VIE TOOK A big bite of one of the gooey, chocolatey brownies she'd made earlier to take to the salon for the Beautiful Day program tomorrow, intending to enjoy the treat while she read her book, just as her phone rang with a call. Mouth full of sticky, sweet goodness, she glanced at the screen to see who it was, hoping she could let it go to voicemail since she wasn't in a position to talk at the moment.

Her stomach did a little happy dance at seeing Eric Miller's name on the display, and since she hadn't heard from him since Friday, she didn't want to miss his call. She tried to swallow the thick brownie at the same time she answered the phone, which, in hindsight, probably wasn't a great idea.

"Hey-roh?" she croaked around the chocolate cake in her throat.

There was a definite pause before Eric spoke. "Hi . . . is this Evie?"

Embarrassment warmed her face, and she gulped again, wishing she had something to drink to help wash down the last of the brownie. "Ummm, 'tis me,"

"Are you okay?" he asked, his tone concerned.

She finally managed to get the majority of the dessert down, at least enough to talk without garbling her words. "I . . . uh . . . I'm good now. I was eating a brownie just as you called and shouldn't have answered the phone with my mouth full."

He chuckled, the sexy sound rippling through her like a physical caress. "Do I need to come over and administer mouth-to-mouth?"

Oh, yes, please, she was tempted to say. All weekend, her mind had replayed what he'd said to her outside of her shop about kissing her— *when it happens, and trust me when I say that it will happen, I want the luxury of taking my time and exploring every inch of your soft, sweet mouth*—and she'd already decided that when and if the opportunity presented itself and he tried to kiss her as part of the whole boyfriend experience, she certainly wasn't going to deny him, or herself.

But right now, she wasn't dressed for company. Her hair was in a sloppy ponytail, she was wearing sleep shorts and a tank top, she had zero makeup on, and she hadn't shaved her legs in, well, almost a month. There had been no reason to . . . until now, just in case her calves or thighs came into contact with any part of Eric at the reunion. Yeah, that was her reasoning and she was sticking to it.

She cleared her throat one last time. "Thank you for the offer, but I think I'm good now."

"Too bad," he murmured, his voice low and teasing. "What are you doing? Other than eating what must have been a very thick, sticky brownie."

The way he said *thick* and *sticky* made her thighs clench. "I'm sitting on my favorite chair in my living room reading a book."

"What kind of book?" he asked curiously.

"A romance novel."

She expected a snarky remark about reading porn, as her ex had referred to her genre preference, and was pleasantly surprised with Eric's reply.

"Ahhh, that's where the guy always gets the girl in the end, right?"

She grinned and switched it up. "Or the girl gets the guy."

"I do love an aggressive woman who knows what she wants and isn't afraid to go after it."

"I'll be sure to remember that." Grinning to herself, she curled her legs beneath her and picked off a very small, safe piece of her brownie and popped it into her mouth. "I'll have you know I'm super aggressive when it comes to the canoe race we always have at the reunion. You'll be my partner, by the way."

"I'll try my best not to disappoint you, but don't get upset if you get wet from all my vigorous . . . rowing."

She laughed, marveling at how comfortable they already were with each other. How easy it was to talk and tease. "What are *you* up to?" she asked, turning the question around on him.

"You do realize, don't you, that question is a loaded one?" His voice was low and husky in her ear. "Do you want the clean answer or the dirty one?"

Evie bit her bottom lip. She was so damn tempted to go the dirty route. "Are you flirting with me, Mr. Miller?"

"Yes, just like any good boyfriend would," he said, his tone amused, though he didn't push on the dirty/clean answer. "So, you mentioned something about your parents being a little over-the-top and I'm going to have to roll with the punches when it comes to them. Care to elaborate on that?"

She groaned, not looking forward to this conversation because she just knew that Eric was going to have a field day with what he learned. But he deserved to know what he was getting himself into so he was prepared when her parents said or did something outlandish. And there was every chance that they would.

"So, yeah, my parents are very open and accepting about just about anything, as long as it doesn't break the law," she said, pinching off another brownie morsel and eating it. "They're also very unconventional, and all about free love and sexual freedom."

He chuckled. "They sound like cool parents to me."

"And extremely embarrassing at times," she added, thinking about the time her father had given her prom date a strip of condoms, "just in case." It had been her senior year and she'd just turned eighteen, as had the guy she'd been with, but at that moment she would have done anything for the floor to open up and swallow her whole.

"My mother is a tantric yoga instructor and

my father is a sexologist." How was that for ridiculously crazy occupations?

"Sexologist?" Eric asked curiously. "What is that?"

"It's a fancy word for sex therapist, but my dad likes to be called a sexologist because he's a specialist in the field. So if my father starts talking to you about erectile dysfunction, or that it's perfectly healthy to fulfill kinky sexual fantasies as long as they're consensual, or my mother takes you aside to let you know what position is the best for a woman to achieve a vaginal orgasm, I'm apologizing right now."

By the time she was done with those warnings, he was laughing so hard it made her giggle, too. When she'd given her ex the same spiel about her parents, he'd been appalled and made her feel as though her parents were freaks.

"Oh my God, I love them already," Eric said once they'd both stopped laughing.

"Honestly, they're fantastic parents and I had a great childhood because they were so open about communicating with me and my brother, who came out as gay a few years ago. I always felt like I could talk to them about anything, and my friends were jealous of that."

"Me, too," he said, startling her with that

admission. "You're very lucky."

She heard the melancholy in his voice, and a bit of sadness. Before she could ask him about his family and parents, he smoothly changed the subject. And truthfully, this exchange didn't require her to know about his family situation, so she let it slide, though she was extremely curious.

"So, I now know that you like brownies and romance novels, but there are other basic things I should know about you if we've been dating a few months, like what is your favorite food?"

"Mmmm. Pepperoni and mushroom pizza with extra cheese." Her mouth watered just mentioning it. "You?"

"Anything Mexican, but if I had to pick only one thing, it would be a chile relleno."

She made an ick sound and a face to go with it, even though he couldn't see her expression. "I can't stand those green chile peppers."

"I'll be sure not to kiss you after I've eaten one," he promised, interjecting the comment so naturally, as if they'd already kissed a dozen times. Or he planned to, anyway. "What's your favorite kind of music?"

"Country."

"Mine's rock."

She shook her head at their different tastes. "Looks like we're going to be fighting over radio stations on the drive to Santa Barbara."

He chuckled. "Are you a dog or cat person?"

"Cat person." Dogs made her nervous. "I had the sweetest cat growing up and I'm thinking of adopting one just to have some company when I'm home."

He groaned in disappointment. "I hate cats. It's a good thing that opposites attract, right?"

"Yes," she agreed, though since they weren't *really* dating, those things weren't an issue.

"Now this question is *really* important," he said, his serious tone grabbing her attention. "What kind of underwear do you prefer to wear?"

She was quiet for a few seconds, the flirty question making her squirm on the couch. She thought about the panties she liked best, bought more for comfort than seduction, and knew if she was honest with her reply, Eric was going to be extremely let down. "Are you sure that question is really necessary?" she asked, keeping her voice light and amused.

"Of course it is. As your boyfriend, I would know this," he said playfully. "Wait. Let me guess."

"Okay." She waited for him to follow that up with a standard male response, like a thong or g-string.

"I think you're all about comfort, but you like pretty, too," he mused. "So, I'm going to go with soft white cotton panties trimmed in lace."

She blinked in shock, wondering how he could have known. "I'm impressed. You're right. Have you been in my lingerie drawer?"

He chuckled, the sound huskier now. "No, but I'm glad I was right. That's the best kind of underwear on a woman."

He was full of surprises, because in her experience, most men wanted to see the barely there panties. "How so?"

"The cotton makes them demure, the hint of lace makes them subtly sexy, so when they're being pulled down a woman's legs, it's like unwrapping a sweet gift that ends up being really fucking hot."

The last part came out as a sexy growl, and Evie's entire body flooded with heat. Her nipples tightened and tingled, and between her legs . . . her neglected lady parts pulsed with an overwhelming desire and need. She could easily imagine him sliding her panties down her legs, his dark, hooded gaze brazenly staring at the treasure he revealed.

She swallowed hard. "Ahhh, I think we need to stop right there," she said, before she spontaneously combusted from his words alone.

"Just for the record, I wear boxer briefs," he offered casually, as if he hadn't just left her completely breathless.

She groaned as an image of Eric in tight black boxer briefs and nothing else filled her mind. "I didn't need to know that." Because now, when she tried to fall asleep, that particular vision would undoubtedly keep her awake and very restless.

"Well, now you do," he said, the wicked note to his voice letting her know he'd deliberately provoked her. "One last important question before I let you go. Are you a girl who likes sweet talk or dirty talk?"

She covered her face with her free hand, feeling it warm beneath her palm. "Why is *that* important?"

"It's *very* important, because your boyfriend should know the best way to seduce you."

God, he was killing her. Eric Miller might not be her legitimate boyfriend, but she wasn't averse to the idea of him doing hot, decadent things to her. And because they weren't face-to-face, she felt bold enough to admit the truth. "Well, not that I've had a whole lot of experience with this, but I'm not opposed to dirty talk."

"Good answer, sweetheart." His low, sexy voice made her shiver.

She bit her bottom lip and dared to ask, "Are you *trying* to seduce me?"

"Only if you want me to," he said, leaving the possibility up to her. "Good night, Evie."

"Night," she whispered. She disconnected the call, but one crucial thought lingered. Did she *want* him to seduce her?

It was crazy because she hadn't known him for very long, but their connection was strong, as was their attraction, and he was the perfect rebound guy after the way her ex had dumped her. She knew up front that they were a temporary item with an end date. She'd hired him for a weekend of the boyfriend experience, bought and paid for . . . well, not paid for yet, but she intended to settle that issue before they left. But the fact that she was aware that the boyfriend gig was a side job for him—a service that pretty much meant he enjoyed his single status—made it easy for her to guard her emotions and keep things between them light and fun, with no messy involvements.

She'd always put her whole heart into relationships, but for once in her life, she just wanted to give in to that no-strings-attached lust and attraction instead of saving it all for a guy who'd only end up letting her down or hurting her in the long run. And at least with Eric, she knew the score and rules up front.

Her stomach danced with anticipation, giving her the answer she sought. If the situation or opportunity presented itself with Eric, she was all in for a weekend of feel-good sex.

CHAPTER SEVEN

A T ONE THIRTY Monday afternoon, Eric parked his car in an open spot near Evie's Beauty and Bliss Salon and Spa. Even though she wasn't expecting him, he had a legit reason for stopping by. And no, he wasn't stalking her.

After last night, he'd gone to bed with a smile on his face, and that hadn't happened in forever and never on a Sunday night after time spent with his mother. But Evie had given him exactly what he needed last night and made him forget about the pain of his sister's death and his family issues.

He had to admit that he enjoyed flirting with her, and if he had his way, they'd be doing a lot more than indulging in sexy banter when they were together. First on his agenda was stealing a kiss. And from there, he'd take his cues from her to see if they were on the same page when it came to taking their attraction to the next level.

Getting out of his car, he headed toward the salon, and as soon as he stepped inside, he was taken aback by all the women in the place and the amount of noise that greeted him—a combination of lively female chatter and happy laughter. The sitting area off to the side of the reception desk was filled with over a dozen clients who appeared to be waiting for an appointment while conversing with the other ladies and enjoying beverages and a table filled with various desserts.

It was a very different scene from the quieter one he'd encountered on Friday, when there had only been one client for each of the women working in the salon. Today, it appeared like he'd walked into a social gathering of some sort.

As soon as the women realized that a man had entered the establishment, the conversations died down, and they all looked at him a little warily, which he found odd. He offered them a friendly smile, then glanced toward Evie's station just as she turned her head to see what had caused the sudden hush that had fallen over the shop.

She saw him and her eyes went wide with surprise. The delighted smile that immediately appeared on her lips made him feel a little sucker-punched, because he knew it was meant just for him. He gave her a small wave, and she said something to the client sitting in her chair, then made her way over to the reception area.

The group of females was still watching him tentatively as Evie approached where he was standing. As soon as she reached him, she turned her attention to the women for a moment.

"It's okay, ladies," she said, her tone light and gentle. "He's a friend of mine."

He was struck by how weird the situation was. Why did Evie have to reassure these women and clarify who he was? But as soon as she did, a collective sense of relief spread throughout the salon and the ladies gradually went back to visiting with each other.

She met his gaze again, her pretty blue eyes filled with unmistakable pleasure. "Hey, what are you doing here?" she asked, not explaining the strange scene he'd just encountered. "Were you in the neighborhood and couldn't resist stopping by to see me?"

She was teasing him, and he liked it. "That's definitely one of the reasons."

Her cheeks flushed a light shade of pink. "And the other?"

"Well, I was hoping you might have room in your schedule to give me a haircut." He ran his fingers through the strands that were longer than he normally let them get, and while he could have gone to his barber, the thought of feeling Evie's fingers running through his hair kind of turned him on. "I don't want to meet your parents looking like a bum, but you obviously have a full day of appointments," he said, referencing all the women in the shop.

"Today is definitely a crazy day," she agreed. "Normally, we're closed on Mondays. We're only open today because of the Beautiful You program, which we do on the last Monday of the month. That's why it's so crowded in here."

She indicated a sign set up on an easel by the front door that said *Welcome to Beautiful You Day!* It didn't explain what the program was, but clearly these women were at the salon and spa to be pampered in some way.

"I'll tell you what," she went on. "If you're willing to come back around six thirty this evening, which is after my last appointment for the day, I'd be happy to give you a haircut."

"Okay, that works for me," he said, and knowing she had clients to attend to, he didn't want to take up any more of her time. "You get back to your customer, and I'll see you in a few hours."

"Sounds good," she said, her eyes sparkling happily. "I'll see you then."

After leaving the shop, Eric drove back to the office for the afternoon, and between fires he and Leo had to put out, phone calls, and paperwork, the time passed quickly. When he returned to Beauty and Bliss at the designated time, the only person left in the salon was Evie. The place was cleaned up, like none of it had ever happened.

"Hey," Evie greeted him from where she was by her station. "Mind locking the door behind you? We're officially closed for the evening, thank goodness."

She sounded exhausted, but she was smiling, like the day had been a good one. He turned the lock to secure the door, then walked over to her. "Thanks for making time for me. I really appreciate it."

"It's not a problem," she said, waving away his thanks. "It's nice and quiet in here now, and your haircut shouldn't take very long. Have a seat in my chair."

He sat down, and as she grabbed the black hair-cutting cape and attached it around his neck, her stomach growled, long and loud.

She laughed in embarrassment. "Well, that was obnoxious."

He chuckled. "Have you had anything to eat?"

"Nothing substantial since breakfast," she said with a shake of her head as she lifted the lid on the cabinet in front of them, revealing a shampoo bowl beneath. "It's been one customer after another all day. I'll grab something after we're done here."

"I'm actually hungry, too. How about I order us a pepperoni and mushroom pizza with extra cheese?" Yeah, he was shamelessly suggesting her favorite food.

She met his gaze, her eyes dancing playfully. "You really *are* trying to seduce me, aren't you?"

"Maybe," he said with a wink, and taking that as a yes, he brought his phone out in front of him and opened up his favorite pizza delivery app.

"While you're doing that, I need to get some towels," she said. "I'll be right back."

By the time she returned, the order was placed. She turned his chair around, lowered the back part, and started shampooing his hair so she could cut it wet. Her nails lightly scratching against his scalp felt amazing . . . and the view he had looking up at her wasn't bad, either. She was wearing a formfitting black T-shirt with the wording *Beautiful You* stamped across her breasts, and as she leaned over him from the side, they came precariously close to brushing against the side of his cheek.

If he could have turned his head, he would have . . . because then he'd be positioned perfectly to bury his face in her full, generous tits. Unfortunately, all he could do was ogle them, and she must have felt his heated stare because her nipples tightened against the cotton fabric of her shirt.

She quickly finished rinsing his hair, towel dried the strands, then sat him back up. When she lowered the top of the cabinet, he could see her standing behind him in the mirror's reflection. The adorable flush on her skin and the way she was biting her lower lip told him she was trying to ignore the way her body had just reacted to him.

She combed through his wet hair and met his gaze in the mirror, hers apologetic. "I'm really sorry about what happened when you stopped by the shop earlier."

He knew exactly what she was referring to.

"Did I do or say something to make all those women uncomfortable?" he asked, because he still had no idea why they'd reacted so strangely when he'd walked into the salon.

"Not you, specifically," she said, using her shears to cut a good inch off of the ends of his hair. "I'm pretty sure they would have reacted that way to any man who walked in, because for one thing, men aren't allowed at the Beautiful You program, and for another, all those women you saw here today are survivors of domestic violence."

"Shit." He couldn't contain his shock. "I'm so sorry. I had no idea . . ."

"Of course you didn't know," she rushed to assure him. "I'm pretty sure when they saw you walk in, their first thought was that you were an abusive boyfriend or husband looking for one of the women in the salon. They were staring at you because they were nervous."

Jesus, now it all made sense. The immediate hush, the wary looks, and why Evie had alleviated the tension in the place by letting all those ladies know that he was a friend of hers. That he wasn't a threat to any of them. He couldn't imagine what any of those women had gone through in their personal lives, but clearly Evie was trying to do something nice for them.

"Tell me about this Beautiful You program," he asked, genuinely interested.

"It's my pet project and baby," she said, her voice filled with pride. "The program is something I started about a year ago. I wanted to find a way to give back to the community, and I had a new client come in who worked at the local women's shelter. By the time I was done with her hair, after hearing all the horrors of what those women went through, I knew I wanted to do something special for them, which led to creating the Beautiful You program."

He watched more of his hair fall to the floor as she continued lifting the strands with a comb and snipping. "How does the program work?"

"Like I told you earlier today, it's the last Monday of the month. So during that month, I'm in contact with the women's shelter to set up appointments for whoever they feel needs a day of pampering, and Scarlett and Jessica and I make sure we accept new women every month to spread the love, so to speak." She smiled as she talked and trimmed around his ears and neck, clearly able to multitask. "We don't charge for any of the services, and everyone leaves with a gift bag filled with beauty products, because most of them don't have much at all. My goal when I first started the program was to make sure that every woman who came into our shop on the Beautiful You day walked out feeling confident and beautiful and knowing that they deserve to be treated like a queen."

He was truly in awe of her selfless, altruistic nature, as well as how passionate she was about the cause. "That's really incredible."

"I really do love doing it every month because it's so rewarding." Done with the cutting part of his hair, she set her comb and scissors aside and reached into a cupboard for a blow-dryer. "The program has been so successful that it caught the attention of the San Diego Chamber of Commerce, and I found out last month that I've been nominated for this year's Humanitarian Award. They'll be presenting me with the award in a few weeks, but what I'm so grateful for is that it puts a spotlight on the issue of domestic violence."

"The award is well deserved," he said, meaning it.

"Thanks," she murmured, a bit shy with compliments.

She turned on the blow-dryer, which made conversation difficult. Five minutes later, she shut it off and he had a great haircut in a fashionably mussed style.

"Looks great," he said as she took off the cape and shook it out. "Thank you."

She smiled at him. "You're welcome."

He got up from the chair, and she picked up a nearby broom and started sweeping up the hair she'd cut. "What do I owe you?" He reached toward his back pocket for his wallet.

She shook her head. "It's no charge."

"Evie, you've spent the entire day cutting people's hair without getting paid. Let me at least pay for mine."

She gave him a direct look. "I'm not taking your money," she insisted as she swept the pile of hair into a dustpan and dumped it into the trash. "Consider it part of me hiring you for next weekend, and speaking of which, we need to discuss your fee."

A loud knock sounded on the glass door, an interruption that Eric was grateful for because he didn't intend to let her pay him a dime for doing something he wanted to do. "Ahhh, dinner's here," he said, and walked to the door with her following.

"This conversation isn't over," she said firmly.

He grinned at her. "It is for now, because we're both starving, and getting food in our stomachs is a priority."

"Fair enough," she replied agreeably, clearly favoring pizza over monetary talk.

Since Eric had paid for their dinner and tipped the delivery guy through the app, he accepted the medium-sized pizza box and the extra item he'd also ordered, and Evie relocked the door, then led the way back to the storage room, where there was an area set up with a table and chairs for employee breaks, he assumed.

She grabbed two bottles of water from a small refrigerator. "What's in the bag?" she asked curiously as she joined him at the table.

"Dessert."

Her eyes lit up with delight, and he loved that she was so unabashed about enjoying sweets. "What kind of dessert?"

"You'll have to wait and see." He set the treat aside and opened the pizza box, and they both inhaled the savory scent of pepperoni, mushrooms, and red sauce and tons of cheese.

They both dug in, using the paper plates and napkins the delivery driver had included. Her first bite in and she was moaning, her eyes rolling back in ecstasy.

He raised a brow in amusement, even while his dirty mind wondered if she'd make those same sounds and that same look during sex. "That good, huh?"

"Oh my God. I'm in heaven," she admitted, and smiled impishly at him when she realized how euphoric she'd just been. "It tastes even better because I'm absolutely famished."

Between the two of them, they finished the pizza in no time at all.

Evie wiped her fingers on a napkin, took a drink of her water, then eagerly eyed the sack he'd put aside. "I'm ready for whatever is in that bag."

He chuckled as he closed the lid on the box. "You're so impatient. Are you one of those people who'd eat dessert first if they could?"

She grinned. "Oh, yeah. Absolutely. I have to say, the guys I've dated have never bought me dessert just for the heck of it, so thank you."

"You're welcome." And those other men were idiots. If a little chocolate made a woman happy, then why not indulge her?

After opening the bag, he withdrew a see-through plastic container and set it on top of the closed pizza box between them. She laughed, her eyes sparkling with pure pleasure at seeing the half-dozen brownies he'd bought from the pizza place's dessert menu.

"You are so bad," she said with a shake of her head, even as she reached for one of the treats. "First my favorite pizza, now brownies."

He picked up one of the squares, too, watching as she took a bite of hers and licked away a crumb from the corner of her mouth. "It's all part of my plan to seduce you," he said, winking at her.

Her gaze met his, and there was no mistaking the glimmer of desire in her pretty blue eyes. "It might be working," she replied boldly.

He stared right back at her, making sure she knew he definitely wanted the same thing. "I fucking hope so," he said, his tone low and husky with a hunger that had nothing to do with the dessert and was directly related to her.

The moment between them teemed with promises and expectations, and when she absently scraped her teeth along her bottom lip, it took every ounce of control Eric possessed not to taste that generous mouth for himself. Oh, he certainly intended to, and soon . . . after she enjoyed her brownie.

She finally continued to eat her treat. "These

are really good," she said, the casual comment doing nothing to cut through the thick sexual tension between them.

He ate one of them, and she had two. When they were done, he closed the lid and pushed them toward her. "Take them home so you can enjoy them later."

"Thank you." She leaned back in her chair, her expression turning serious. "We still have something important to discuss," she reminded him.

He relaxed in his seat, too, knowing what that conversation was. "My fee for the weekend?"

She nodded. "Yes. I'd like to get that out of the way before we leave on Friday."

He seriously debated telling her the whole truth, about how he'd been set up on the Boyfriend Experience app by a friend and had been dared to accept her request. That's truly how it all started, and he'd had no intention of actually agreeing to be her boyfriend. But then he'd met her, and between the attraction and her story about her asshole ex and just genuinely liking her, Eric let the misunderstanding slide.

And now, taking monetary payment from her felt wrong, not that he'd ever considered it.

However, coming clean at this point had its drawbacks, as well—most notably the possibility that she'd conclude that she'd misread the whole situation and think *he* was a dickhead for misleading her. He didn't want her to think he'd agreed to be her fake boyfriend because he felt sorry for her when that was the furthest thing from the truth. This woman in front of him had so much pride, and no way did he want to do anything to damage that self-esteem.

The way Eric saw the situation, he was giving her the boyfriend treatment, which was exactly what she wanted, and in return, he was going to enjoy playing the part, so what was the harm?

"That much, huh?" she asked with a disappointed sigh.

Her soft voice pulled him out of his thoughts, making him realize he'd spent way too much time in his head trying to rationalize his actions, to the point that he had no idea how she'd come to any conclusion about his payment.

"What do you mean?" he asked.

A small smile touched the corner of her mouth. "It's taking you forever to answer, so I'm assuming your fee for the weekend is pretty astronomical."

She sounded completely bummed, and he decided to go forward with his idea, which would really benefit them both. Was it risky? Hell yeah, but nothing ventured was nothing gained. "Actually, my fee is pretty reasonable. I want payment for the weekend in kisses."

She narrowed her gaze in confusion. "Excuse me?"

He allowed a sinful smile to hitch up the corners of his mouth. "I want to kiss you, Evie . . . anytime I want."

She looked taken aback and a little wary. "Is that how you collect payment from all your clients?"

It was a fair enough question, and he understood her concern. "You're my first client, sweetheart. The app just started beta testing, remember? So, no, I've never traded in a fee for unlimited amounts of kissing."

Her face flushed, just enough to tell him she was tempted . . . but still skeptical, especially after being duped by her ex. "Why kisses over money?"

Because he didn't need the goddamn money, and because he was dying to get his mouth on hers. It was that simple. Also, he instinctively knew that one kiss with Evie Bennett wouldn't even come close to being enough, so that extra *anytime I want* clause covered the entire weekend.

"Why *not* kisses over money?" he countered. "Shouldn't I be able to choose the form of payment? Unless kissing me is not what *you* want?"

She swallowed hard. "I think I want it too much," she admitted, her voice a soft, vulnerable whisper between them.

"Then we're definitely on the same page," he said, making sure she knew how much he wanted her, as well. "Me wanting to kiss you shouldn't come as a surprise, Evie. I already told you it was going to happen. This just gives me permission to do so anytime I want. Do we have a deal?"

Her breathing deepened as she considered his offer, but the anticipation in her eyes told him she was one hundred percent on board with the idea. "Yes, we have a deal."

Satisfied with her answer, he scooted his chair back to make room for her and wasted no time collecting the debt. "Come here, Evie," he cajoled seductively as he held out his hand to her. "I'd like my down payment now, please."

CHAPTER EIGHT

E VIE WAS CERTAINLY surprised that Eric had
waived his Boyfriend Experience fee for
unlimited kisses, but after his persuasive argu-
ment, she'd concluded that it was his
prerogative to ask for whatever payment he
deemed worth his time. Wanting to kiss her
meant he was attracted to her, and the thought
made her body hum with pleasure. And truthfully, who was she to complain when she'd
already decided during their conversation last
night that if the opportunity to kiss Eric presented itself, she wasn't going to turn him
down?

Her stomach was already fluttering with excitement as she stood up and rounded the table
to him. She placed her hand in his bigger,
warmer one, and he drew her closer. She
expected him to position her across his lap . . .
but instead he guided her in front of where he
was sitting. He looked up at her, meeting her

gaze as he let go of her hand. His sexy smile stole her breath as he ran his palms up over the curve of her hips until his fingers gripped her waist.

"Straddle my thighs, Evie," he said, a gentle but firm order as he deliberately nudged her legs apart with his knees.

With her heart galloping wildly in her chest, she followed his order and settled herself so she was sitting astride his lap, her thighs spread to accommodate his hips and her hands braced on his shoulders. They were face-to-face, and the heat in his eyes started a slow, melting sensation inside her.

He skimmed his palms lower, until they were cupping her ass, his fingers splayed wide. "I want you closer," he murmured, and effortlessly guided her up the few inches separating them, until her breasts brushed against his chest and she could feel the solid ridge of flesh beneath his slacks notched right up against the inner seam of her jeans. Her clit pulsed shamelessly at the teasing pressure.

The position was so intimate and so damn arousing that she couldn't hold back the pleasurable gasp that escaped her.

He smirked knowingly. "You good?"

She managed a jerky nod, trying not to grind herself against him like a brazen hussy. "Yeah . . . very good."

"It's about to get a whole lot better." He framed her face in his hands, gently but firmly, while his thumb swept across her damp bottom lip. "I'm going to make you forget all about your idiot ex," he promised as he brought her slowly, inexorably, toward the temptation that beckoned.

He'd already been doing just that, but she shivered, her nipples puckering hard and tight as he deliberately drew out the anticipation of their first kiss. She stared into the rich depths of his eyes, then let her gaze drop to his full, inviting lips. Their faces were so close she could see the hint of stubble on his jaw, could feel his warm breath caress her cheek. The wanting increasing inside her made her shift restlessly on his lap.

Frustrated noises rumbled up from her throat and she slid her hands down to his chest, gathering the fabric of his shirt in her fists. "Eric . . . I'm seduced," she told him, admitting what he'd so easily managed. "Kiss me already."

"Not completely seduced," he said huskily, running his tongue along her lower lip and sucking the soft, tender flesh into his mouth until she moaned. "But you will be by the time we're done. Hang on, Evie. This is going to be one helluva wild ride."

His mouth finally took hers, stealing her breath and senses at the same time. He slid past her parted lips, and she welcomed him eagerly, their tongues tangling erotically. His fingers slid deeper into her hair, gripping the strands and tilting her head to the side to slant his lips more completely over hers. He tasted like the best kind of sin, along with a hint of something more dangerously addictive. It was exhilarating and a bit frightening, considering she had no business letting any kind of long-term craving form with this man.

But the truth couldn't be ignored . . . with just a kiss, she wanted more. Needed more . . . like his mouth in intimate places, his fingers touching and stroking and appeasing the ache throbbing at the crux of her thighs. And the undeniable erection making itself known between them . . . the thought of him burying his cock to the hilt inside her caused Evie to whimper against his lips.

Desire, hot and molten, spiraled down to her core, and the unexpected intensity of it made her head spin. So much passion, so quickly, defied reason because no man had ever turned her on this fast or set her body on fire with just a kiss. And the knowledge that he was equally aroused because of her was exhilarating.

His mouth continued to consume hers, edgy and hungry and blissfully indulgent, and after a good long while, his lips separated from hers and he tugged her head farther back so he could trail hot, damp, suctioning kisses down the side of her neck. His soft tongue licked a path to her collarbone, then back up to below her ear, where he nipped just hard enough to make her entire body jolt from that wicked, breathtaking bite against her skin.

There was no holding back her soft cry of pleasure that sounded incredibly sexual and needy.

"You taste so fucking good," he rasped against her ear, his voice pure, liquid sex. "I could eat you up. Every inch of you."

His hot, perfect words made her shudder against him and set her ablaze. Everywhere. He was giving her the dirty-talk treatment. And coming from him, she liked it. A lot.

He went in for a second kiss, their mouths coming together for another long, thrilling make-out session, until they were both precariously close to doing something she wasn't sure she was ready for . . . yet. And definitely not at her workplace.

As if he sensed where her mind had drifted, he slowly, gradually let their lips separate. They were both panting for breath, and he pressed his forehead against hers, giving them both time to recover. After a few moments, he tipped her head back until her gaze met his dark, approving one.

"I think my world just tilted on its axis a bit," he murmured, grinning.

She laughed softly, because she knew Eric was teasing her. But right now, with her heart racing in her chest and her own emotions a bit topsy-turvy, she didn't want to admit that she'd felt that shift, too. For real.

FOR THE REST of the week, Evie didn't see Eric because of their busy schedules leading up to the holiday weekend, but they did text often. Mostly funny comments or questions about the reunion and a few flirty messages from Eric, but she was grateful that she'd had a few days to pull herself together after that unraveling kiss at the salon on Monday night. The one that felt and tasted like a whole lot more than a down payment for his services.

According to his messages, he was already anticipating his next "fee." Honestly, so was Evie, because the man had a mouth on him that was sex personified and made her want to do all sorts of bad, naughty things to him and with him. Like tear off his clothes so she could have her wicked way with his gorgeous, drool-worthy body, she thought as she finished the last of her packing. She just had to be smart about the situation and keep in mind that this was nothing more than a temporary arrangement. She wasn't looking to get involved with anyone anytime soon, and clearly that wasn't on his agenda, either, considering his presence on a dating type app.

She'd decided this weekend was all about having fun with Eric, and if something more happened between them, which was likely, given their explosive chemistry, she'd just have to keep her emotions in check and her heart to herself. Simple enough, she told herself. Not that she really believed it.

A half an hour later, she was rolling her

small suitcase out to the entry area of her apartment when her doorbell rang. Even though she was fairly certain it was Eric picking her up for their four-hour trip to Santa Barbara—he'd insisted on driving and she appreciated the offer because his car was far more luxurious than hers—she checked the peephole, just to be sure. He stood on the other side on her little porch, grinning at her, then waggled his brows lasciviously. She laughed, just as he'd no doubt intended, and opened the door. He was certainly amusing and unpredictable, but that playfulness was something she enjoyed about him. She felt like she'd smiled more with Eric in the short time that she'd known him than in all the time she'd been with her ex.

"Hey, beautiful," he said, making her blush at the greeting while his gaze took in the summer dress and sandals she was wearing.

She wanted to tell him that compliments weren't necessary, but he didn't look like he was paying lip service for the sake of being her pretend boyfriend, and since there was no one else around, he clearly meant what he said. The genuine appreciation in his sexy green eyes was honest and real, and it felt good to be the object of a man's desire.

He stepped inside, and without giving her the chance to close the door, he framed her face in his hands, tipped her head back, and kissed her... deliciously soft, incredibly slow, and arousingly deep. With a low moan of pleasure, she placed her hands on his chest and fell headlong into the delightful bliss of his lips sliding against hers and his tongue teasing and cajoling her to play.

It was the best kind of hello, and by the time he lifted his mouth and ended the leisurely kiss, her entire body felt pliant and desire spilled through her veins.

"Ummm," he murmured, nipping gently at her bottom lip, that small tug of his teeth making her nipples bloom hard and tight against the front of her dress. "I missed you."

Her breath caught, until she realized that he must have meant he missed *kissing* her. That certainly made more sense, she thought, smiling up at him. "I suppose that's a good thing, considering you're stuck with me for the next four days."

"I'm looking forward to every minute of it," he said with one of those sexy winks before finally releasing her.

"You haven't met my crazy parents yet," she

said, then added beneath her breath, "Or my spiteful cousin."

He arched a brow. "Now that sounds like a conversation we should have on the drive."

Ugh. It was a discussion she absolutely dreaded, but no way did she want Eric to meet Raquel without knowing all the facts up front so he knew what he was dealing with. Her cousin was the queen of zingers, barbs, and underhanded, sly insinuations when it came to Evie.

She reached for the handle on her carry-on-size luggage, but Eric beat her to it.

"Is this the only bag you have?" he asked, looking around for others.

She laughed. "Yes. We're going to a camping resort, not Paris."

"I just thought women needed more . . . stuff when they traveled. You know, makeup, hair products, and enough clothes to change outfits three times a day."

Clearly, the women he'd gone on trips with were high maintenance compared to her. Probably more sophisticated, too. She pushed aside the twist of jealousy at the notion of him being with other women. "There's plenty of *stuff* in there. We're only going to be at the resort for three days, and shorts, T-shirts, and a bathing suit don't take up much room."

Interest lit his green eyes, and a slow, sinful smile curved his lips. "One-piece or two?"

He was such a typical male and she refrained from rolling her eyes at his question. "I'm sorry to disappoint you, but it's a one-piece. I don't do bikinis." She didn't have the kind of body she'd ever flaunt in public.

"I don't know why you'd think I'd be disappointed. A one-piece bathing suit can be provocative and sexy as hell." The words came out on a possessive, toe-curling growl. "And just for the record, I don't want your boobs hanging out of a tiny bikini top for other guys to lust over when you're mine for the weekend. Besides, there's something to be said for leaving something to a guy's imagination."

She shook her head at him. "You are such an anomaly."

He caught his fingers beneath her chin and tipped her head back to keep her gaze on his. "No, not really. You just need to fucking own this incredible body of yours, including rocking the hell out of a one-piece."

God, fake boyfriend or not, he was so good for her confidence. "We need to get going," she said, not sure what else to say to his last remark.

He held her gaze for a long moment more, then finally let his fingers fall away as they exited her apartment. She locked everything up behind them, and he led the way to his dark gray BMW. She still didn't fully understand how he could afford such a high-end vehicle working as a chauffeur, but regardless, she settled into the leather passenger seat that felt like butter against her skin and buckled up. Everything inside the car was so luxurious she felt as though she was traveling in first class.

As he navigated the way toward the freeway, he deemed her his copilot, which meant letting her have free rein of his satellite radio. It was all so new to her when she'd only ever used a regular radio and a cd player, but a short while later, she found a station that played contemporary country music, and after a few songs played, he openly admitted to liking the songs and artists.

"So, a small change of plans for this evening," she said as they finally made their way out of the busy, early-afternoon San Diego freeway traffic. "My mother called to let me know that she already checked us into our cabin. Since none of the reunion stuff starts until tomorrow morning at breakfast, we're meeting my parents for dinner before heading to the resort if that's okay?"

"Of course," he said easily.

She glanced over at him sitting in the driver's seat, admiring his gorgeous profile. "They're very excited to finally meet you . . . the other Eric . . . well, you know what I mean," she said, because the whole thing seemed so confusing.

He smiled at her. "Evie, don't sweat the small stuff. We got this."

His voice was soft and so reassuring, and the way he said *we got this* with such conviction made it feel as though they were a real couple. When she'd hired him, all she'd wanted was a guy to stand in as her boyfriend so she didn't have to be the single, recently dumped one at the reunion when her cousin would undoubtedly be flaunting her recent engagement. But as they headed into this family gathering, he made her feel confident and secure because, crazily enough, she trusted him. She knew that no matter what came her way this weekend, this man would have her back. She couldn't say that she would have felt that same way if it had been her ex accompanying her.

"So, let's talk about this spiteful cousin of

yours," he said, bringing up the one thing she had no desire to talk about, but Raquel was a big part of the reason she'd hired Eric to be her boyfriend, so it needed to be discussed.

The situation between the two of them was complicated, and she figured it was best to start from the beginning so he had all the inside information and he'd be able to meet her cousin with his eyes wide open and knowing what Raquel was capable of.

"My cousin Raquel is my dad's brother's daughter," she said, letting that sink in for a moment so he knew which side of the family she was referring to. "We're the same age, born the same year . . . but out of the two of us, I was always my grandfather's favorite and I really think it had more to do with me spending more of my time with him than Raquel ever did. She never had the desire or the patience, so he doted on me because I was always hanging around him. Raquel was the beauty queen and cheerleader growing up, and I was the tomboy who loved going fishing with my grandpa. I loved listening to his stories, while she'd roll her eyes and walk away. I played checkers and chess and backgammon with my grandfather Randall, and Raquel had no interest in bonding with him in any way unless it benefitted her. And the closer my grandpa and I got, the more jealous Raquel became."

"Which sounds ridiculous and petty since she clearly made no effort to get her fair share of attention," Eric summed up accurately, his tone droll.

"Exactly," she agreed. "Raquel has always been very spoiled by her parents, and she wanted that attention in materialistic things and not in time spent with Grandpa Randall. As the years went on, her resentment grew, and she decided to punish me for having a great relationship with our grandfather."

He cast her a quick, curious look. "How so?"

"First, it started with snide comments, usually having to do with how I dressed compared to her or what she had that I didn't, not that any of that honestly mattered to me. We went to the same high school, and that's when it got worse. She started stupid, embarrassing rumors about me. She did things in the hallway or classrooms to humiliate me in front of my friends and put me down in sly, underhanded ways. It was . . . rough," she said, hating those years in school because of her cousin's bullying tactics.

"Why didn't you say something to your parents about what she was doing?" Eric asked, his tone sympathetic, which made her cringe inside because she didn't want him feeling sorry for her. "I'm sure if they'd known how Raquel was treating you, they would have talked to your aunt and uncle about the situation and put a stop to it."

She breathed out. "I did tell them. Once. When I was about thirteen and she'd put gum in my hair after I just had it cut in a pretty new style that I loved," she said, recalling the painful event that had resulted in her having to chop another four inches off the length of the hair she'd so painstakingly grown out for two years, all because the glob of gum had been so badly matted in the strands. "My aunt and uncle asked Raquel what happened, and she claimed it was all an accident and I was being a tattletale because I wanted to get her in trouble."

"Jesus Christ," he said, angry on her behalf. "How does someone *accidentally* put gum in someone's hair?"

"I'm not sure, but Raquel managed to convince them she had," she said. "So, after that, knowing my aunt and uncle wouldn't do anything to stop her behavior, I just did my best to avoid her whenever I could."

She paused for a moment, twisting her fingers anxiously in her lap before getting the rest of the story out in the open. "After high school, I went to beauty school to get my cosmetology license because I really liked cutting and styling hair, and that year during a family holiday get-together, Raquel came up to me when no one else was around and said that it was great that I was going to beauty school to make other people as pretty as possible because I understood how it felt to be less than attractive."

She saw Eric's jaw drop open, then snap shut. His fingers tightened on the steering wheel as he glanced at her with a fierce scowl. "She's a fucking piece of work, isn't she?"

His rhetorical question didn't need a response. Evie's stomach twisted into a knot as she gathered the fortitude to share the last and final situation involving her cousin because it was the most critical part of the story. "There's one more important thing you need to know. About five years ago, the two of us were at a wedding for a friend of the family, and there was a good-looking guy there named Graham North, who started talking to me. I was kind of surprised he singled me out, because I was sitting at the same table as my cousin and kept waiting for him to switch his attention to her, because that's what I was used to when it came to men and Raquel," she said with a small laugh. "They always ended up choosing her over me.

"She attempted to flirt with him, and while Graham was polite to her, he was genuinely interested in me, which made her furious, because guys did not ignore someone as beautiful as Raquel. Even after Graham and I started dating, at family functions she'd single him out and didn't hesitate to tease him or touch him or laugh in that coquettish way that grated on my nerves because I knew she wanted nothing more than to have Graham break up with me for her."

The nausea in her stomach increased, and she pushed through it. "Graham and I were together for almost three years, and I thought we'd end up getting married. After graduating with my cosmetology license, I worked at a salon in Fresno, and I was at the shop long hours because I was trying to build my clientele, but at the end of our time together, I started noticing that Graham was becoming emotionally distant and withdrawn, and when I made time for us to spend together, he always had an excuse as to why he was busy. He started working out, which was something he'd never done in the past, as well as dressing differently, and just . . . changing into a guy who was overly concerned with his looks. He texted and called less often. Sex became nonexistent, which he blamed on my work schedule, and I started feeling so guilty about everything, like I was letting him down."

The song "Before He Cheats" by Carrie Underwood played in the background, and she almost laughed at the timing and irony of the fitting lyrics.

"How did you find out?" Eric asked somberly, obviously knowing where her story was heading and how it would end.

"I decided to make him dinner on a Saturday night so we'd have some quality time together, in hopes of getting things back on track," she said, staring ahead at the cars in front of theirs on the freeway. "He came over, but when I tried to hug and kiss him hello, it felt so painfully awkward . . .and I remember thinking that whatever the issue was, it wasn't me. It was him. He wasn't making any effort to be affectionate or meet me halfway in my attempts to make our relationship work."

She rubbed her fingers along her forehead and forced herself to finish. "While I was setting the table, he went to the bathroom, and his phone, which he'd left on the table, lit up with a message. I just happened to glance at it because it was right in front of me, and the display showed a text from Raquel asking him what time he was coming over later that night."

Eric swore beneath his breath and reached out and grabbed her hand, telling her without words just how sorry he was. His touch had such a calming effect on her, and as much as she liked it, she knew better than to get used to it.

"Yeah . . . I'll admit I did *not* see that one coming." Back then, she'd been devastated. Now, she just hated that she'd wasted three years on an unfaithful asshole. "When I confronted Graham, he got defensive about it, and somehow it became *my* fault that he put *his* dick in *my* cousin," she said in a droll tone, trying to disguise the hurt she was feeling.

An abrupt gust of laughter escaped Eric, and she smiled, which helped to ease the knot that had tightened in her stomach.

"So, after I kicked him out, I made the decision to move away from Fresno, because I needed to start my life somewhere new where I didn't have to deal with my cousin or see her with Graham." Evie shivered at the soothing way Eric rubbed his thumb along the back of her hand. "I decided on San Diego, and Scarlett and Jessica, who worked at the same place as I did in Fresno, decided they wanted to join me."

"For real?" he asked with a surprised grin.

She nodded. "My parents were supportive and excited that I was doing something so adventurous, and when I told my grandpa, he was happy for me, too. He also surprised me with a small trust fund he'd set aside for all of his grandkids. He said that he hadn't told any of the grandkids about the money, because he wanted to be able to give it to us when we needed it the most and not because we thought we deserved it. And he was adamant that the money would be an investment in my future. So, off I went to San Diego, and Jessica and Scarlett and I were lucky enough to find an older woman who was looking to sell her salon because she wanted to retire, and the three of us went in on the business together."

"And this is where you live happily ever after, right?" he teased lightheartedly.

"Not quite," she murmured. "Don't forget

about cheater number two, who pretty much crushed my faith in the opposite sex," she said, injecting a joking note in her tone. She wasn't trying to put down the man sitting beside her in any way, but it was easy to be open and honest with Eric since they weren't technically dating. "For now, I think I just need to be single for a while and figure out why my judgment in men sucks so badly."

He squeezed her hand, which to her was much more comforting than platitudes or pity. She didn't need to be on the receiving end of *you're better off without him* or *you deserve better.* Between Graham and her latest ex, she'd heard enough of those sympathetic comments to last her a lifetime.

"This reunion is the first time I'll see both of them since moving to San Diego. They just got engaged, so I'm prepared to have that flaunted in my face, too." She sighed, feeling mentally and emotionally exhausted after reliving the past, and she glanced over at him as he kept his eyes on the road. "And now, knowing all the drama that you're probably going to get sucked into, are you sure you don't want to request a monetary fee for your time?" she asked, more than a little serious.

He flashed her a sinful, toe-curling grin. "Sweetheart, you underestimate just how much I enjoy kissing you. There's not a chance in hell I'm giving up that privilege for a paycheck."

To her surprise, he lifted her hand to his mouth and brushed his lips across her knuckles, so gently, so sweetly she melted inside.

"There's one thing I can promise you this weekend," he went on, determination in his voice. "Your entire family is going to think you have a fucking amazing boyfriend who absolutely adores you. And your cousin and Graham? They're both going to see that, despite what happened, you've moved on to much better things. *Me* being that much better thing," he added, winking at her.

She laughed, and all the dread, anxiety, and insecurities that had been creeping up on her in regard to seeing Graham and Raquel together again seemed to drift away because Eric was right. She did have more exciting and fun things to focus on this weekend, like enjoying the whole boyfriend experience and everything Eric decided it would entail. Being the center of his attention. Indulging in his flirtatious banter. Basking in all the spontaneous kissing.

And just being herself around him, no pretenses or measuring up to someone else's standards, because there were no expectations between them. The thought of being comfortable in her own skin for a change and not trying so hard to be an ideal woman for a guy who didn't care in the end, anyway, was immensely appealing.

Except she couldn't help but feel a stab of disappointment at the thought of her and Eric going their separate ways after what was destined to be an exceedingly enjoyable weekend.

CHAPTER NINE

WITH THE GPS announcing that they were ten minutes away from their destination, which was the restaurant where he and Evie were meeting her parents for dinner, he glanced over at the woman who was sleeping so soundly in the passenger seat. Soon after she'd shared all the ugly details about her relationship with her cousin, she rested her head against the window, and within minutes she'd drifted off to sleep.

He let her doze because she clearly needed the rest and mental and emotional reboot before seeing her parents. He'd heard the pain in her voice when she'd shared everything that had happened with Raquel and then with Graham. The few times he'd glanced at her, he'd witnessed her vulnerability. Opening up to him couldn't have been easy, but the fact that Evie had trusted him with something so hurtful and, yes, humiliating made something odd shift in his chest, which he chalked up to a feeling of protectiveness over her.

He might not have ever put his heart on the line for a woman like Evie had for Graham, and then the other Eric, but he could relate to her pain because his sister's death had devastated him, shattered his family, and left him feeling isolated and alone. Which was why he'd avoided getting emotionally attached to a woman—he feared the potential loss or breakup would take him back to that place he never wanted to relive again. There was also that nagging thought in the back of his mind that revisited him now and then . . . Since his twin had died of cancer at such a young age, couldn't that happen to him considering they shared the same genetic makeup?

Some might call it ridiculous; others might validate his concerns. Clearly, he had commitment issues, and it had always been easier and safer—for himself and the women he dated—to keep relationships casual.

He intended to do just that with Evie this weekend, but he vowed that he wasn't going to let anyone hurt, belittle, or humiliate her on his watch. As far as everyone who looked at the two of them was concerned, Evie lit up his world. His heart gave an odd skip in his chest because there was truth in that statement, and he tried not to think about what would happen after this weekend, when he no longer had an excuse to see her.

Arriving at the diner, he turned into the parking lot and found a vacant spot for his car. He turned off the engine, surprised that Evie remained sleeping. Smiling to himself, he reached across the space between them and gently caressed the back of his hand down her soft cheek, awakening her.

She gradually stirred, making the softest, sexiest sounds that went straight to his dick, and he immediately warded off any dirty thoughts before they blossomed in his mind. Meeting Evie's parents for the first time with a hard-on was not cool.

"Hey, we're here," he said, watching as her eyes fluttered open and she tried to reorient herself as to where she was.

She turned her head to look at him, her blue eyes slumberous and her complexion turning pink in embarrassment. "I can't believe I fell asleep on you. I'm so sorry. That was so rude."

He smiled, still stroking her cheek with his thumb. "No worries. You were tired, and it gave me time to bond with your country music station," he teased. "I'm now a bona-fide fan of Luke Bryan, Jason Aldean, and Carrie Underwood."

She laughed, the warm, husky sound wrapping intimately around him. He wanted to lean over and settle his mouth over hers, but knowing what kissing her did to him, he refrained.

"We should go inside," he said, reluctantly pulling his hand back to his side of the car. "Just in case your parents are already here and waiting for us."

"Okay." She unbuckled her seat belt while he did the same.

They got out of the car, and he came around to her side, closed the door, then slipped his hand securely into hers. He heard her startled intake of breath at the affectionate gesture, and while he could have told her he was playing the part of her boyfriend, the truth was, that would have been a lie. He was holding her hand because he wanted to. Because he enjoyed touching her and having that connection between them.

As soon as they entered the diner, he saw an older couple standing in the lobby, and when the woman saw Evie, her face broke into a huge, happy smile.

"Evie!" she squealed in excitement.

Her mother—Eric assumed—launched herself at Evie, hugging her tight, and he stepped back to let them have their moment.

"Oh my God, I've been so excited to see you!" the other woman said, rocking her daughter back and forth. "Seven months is way too long!"

Eric did the quick math in his head. December. She must have gone home for Christmas . . . *before* dating the other Eric.

As soon as her mom released her, Evie's dad immediately engulfed her in his embrace. "Hey, baby girl," he said affectionately before letting her go.

"Hi, Mom, Dad. It's so good to see you both," Evie said happily, then turned toward Eric to introduce him to her parents. "This is Eric. Eric, this is my mother and father, Lauren and Gene."

As soon as he stepped forward, her mother didn't hesitate to give him the same treatment she'd given her daughter. He found himself wrapped in a hug that was genuinely given, which startled the hell out of him. He wasn't used to random hugs from people he'd just met.

She ended the embrace quickly but looked

up at him with a sassy grin. "I'm a hugger, so get used to it."

Yeah, Lauren was definitely a firecracker, he thought in amusement.

When Eric switched his attention to her dad, Gene thrust out his hand, his eyes dancing with humor. "A handshake will do just fine, son," he said, probably having seen how awkward he'd been with Lauren's overzealous hug.

He appreciated the more masculine greeting and shook the other man's hand. "It's a pleasure to meet you both."

"Likewise," Gene replied.

"Bennett, party of four," the hostess called out.

"Right here," her mother singsonged, waggling her fingers in the air.

As Evie's parents followed the hostess ahead of them, Evie gave Eric an impish look. "See what I mean?" she mouthed to him.

He shook his head. "They're great," he mouthed back to her.

She rolled her eyes, clearly expecting his opinion to change at some point.

They sat down at a table, with Gene and Lauren sitting across from him and Evie. The hostess handed out their menus, and they were all quiet for a few minutes while everyone perused the dinner options. They all ended up ordering regular cheeseburgers with fries, except for Lauren, who opted for a vegan burger.

Once the waiter delivered their drinks, Evie glanced across the table at her mother and father. "I've missed you guys so much," she said, her voice filled with emotion.

"We've missed you, too," her mother said, just as sentimentally.

Then, just as Eric expected, Gene addressed him and the grilling began. "So, Evie tells us that you're a social worker."

"Yes, sir," he said politely, and immediately saw the glint of respect in Gene's eyes at the formal way he'd addressed the other man.

"Mental health and substance abuse, right?" her father continued, clearly wanting to know more about Eric's "career."

During one of their text conversations throughout the week, Evie had told him what kind of social worker her ex was, which had given Eric time to read up on the occupation so he was prepared and he'd know what the hell he was talking about. He couldn't say he was comfortable lying, but that's what this performance was all about. "I work for a public agency and help people with a wide variety of mental health and substance abuse problems. I also participate in outreach and preventative programs."

"That's a very commendable career," Lauren chimed in, sounding impressed.

Yes, considering what a douchebag Evie's ex turned out to be, it was surprising that he'd had such a respectable job that required compassion and empathy—the two things the cheating asshole had lacked when it came to his relationship with Evie.

"And what about your family?" Lauren asked, her eyes filled with curiosity as she took a drink of her iced tea.

Beneath the table, Eric instinctively sought and found Evie's hand. Not questioning why he needed that connection, he entwined their fingers and rested their joined hands on his thigh. Evie had mentioned that her parents knew nothing about ex-Eric's family background and had told him that whatever story he wanted to fabricate, she'd go along with.

"Unfortunately, my parents are divorced," he said, keeping things simple.

"That's always a hard situation," Lauren said

sympathetically.

She had no idea just how difficult, but he nodded in agreement and didn't elaborate.

"Any brothers or sisters?" she asked, changing the subject to one she thought would be less painful than his parents splitting up.

His heart raced at the question, his throat felt tight, and he found himself squeezing Evie's hand. He could have glossed over the truth and just gone with a generic, easy, *I'm an only child* response. But in that moment, he knew he couldn't and wouldn't lie and tarnish his sister's memory. She'd been such a part of him that he'd never deliberately act as though she never existed, even during this pretend situation, when she'd been his other half. He just couldn't do it. And though he realized Evie would be hearing it for the first time now, he felt it was right to reveal.

"I had a twin sister," he said, hearing the sudden rough timbre to his voice and the emotion that was there despite how hard he tried to keep it at bay. "She died of leukemia when we were sixteen."

Lauren's eyes widened in dismay, and beside him, he heard Evie's sharp gasp of shock. Even Gene looked completely taken aback by the unexpected revelation.

"I'm so sorry," Lauren said, her voice soft as she pressed a hand over her heart, her expression as gutted as he felt inside.

"Yes, we are," Gene echoed the sentiment. "That must have been a terrible thing to go through, for you and your parents."

Even though Gene was a sexologist, Eric guessed that the other man probably had a degree, or at least a lot of training in psychology, and knew how traumatizing the event had been. "It was," Eric admitted, completely aware of how Evie now squeezed *his* hand. Letting him know she was there and that she cared. Her quiet support meant everything to him right now.

Thank God the waitress arrived with their burgers, relieving the uncomfortable atmosphere at the table. They all busied themselves with their meals, and after a few bites into their dinners, Lauren spoke, her tone much more upbeat than it had been a couple of minutes ago.

"Being together this weekend is going to be so much fun I can hardly wait!" she said, excitement infusing her voice. "I already have everything planned out, and what's happening when. Of course, everyone will have some free time throughout the day, but there are plenty of activities to keep us all busy and interacting."

Evie glanced at Eric and rolled her eyes. "Every time we do this family reunion, my mother comes prepared with an itinerary."

Lauren smiled at him. "I like to be organized, otherwise it's complete chaos, and this is about making memories with all of the family, which means spending time together," she pointed out. "On Sunday morning, I'm doing a beginners' tantric yoga session for couples, and I fully expect the two of you to be there. Trust me when I say it'll be very beneficial to your sex life."

Evie put her burger down on her plate and groaned in dread. "*Mom,*" she chastised beneath her breath, clearly embarrassed.

Her dad laughed. "If it makes you feel any better, your mother has instructed me to be there, as well, though I'm well versed in all things tantric."

Lauren shimmied her arm against Gene's while giving him a mischievous look. "Oh, yes, you most definitely are well versed." Her voice spilled over with innuendo.

"That does not make me feel better," Evie

replied, shaking her head. "I don't want to watch my parents do anything even remotely sexual."

Evie's mother blinked at her. "There's no actual sex involved in the session, honey. It's all about increasing the connection and intimacy between you and your partner. It's about becoming aware of your body and what gives you the most pleasure."

Evie smacked her forehead with her palm. "Mom . . . just stop."

Eric was grinning, amused by the whole exchange and grateful for the humorous topic. "Sunday. Got it. We'll be there," he told Lauren.

She beamed at him. "Excellent." Then she shifted her gaze to Evie. "See, that wasn't so difficult. At least Eric is excited about the session."

Excited was a gross exaggeration. He was just quickly coming to realize that it was easier if they agreed with Evie's mother instead of fighting the inevitable.

The rest of the dinner conversation was light and superficial. By the end of the meal, Eric decided that he really liked her parents. Were they a little out there? Yes, they were, but ultimately they were a lot of fun and didn't take life too seriously. And it was clear that Gene and Lauren loved each other and their daughter very much. A long-lasting marriage was nice to see for a change.

Gene insisted on paying for the meal, then they all walked out to the parking lot together.

Lauren dug into her purse and withdrew a key with a wooden fob with a number on it, handing it to Evie. "Here's your key since I've already checked you in. And I left a little something for the two of you in your cabin. You know, just to spice things up."

Evie took the key, her cheeks turning a bright shade of pink. "Uhhh, thank you?" she said, her tone a little sarcastic.

"Oh, I'm sure you will." Lauren gave them both an exaggerated wink.

As soon as they were in the car, Evie buried her hands in her face and groaned like a wounded animal. "*Now* do you see how ridiculous my parents are?"

He laughed. "No. I find them . . . fascinating. And I can't wait to see what your mother left for us."

She dropped her hands and stared at him incredulously. "Think extra ribbed condoms, flavored lubricant, handcuffs, a vibrator ... None of those things are beyond the realm of possibility with my mom."

"Now I *really* can't wait." Grinning, he hooked his hand around the back of her neck and drew her face to his so that he was looking into her light, blue eyes. They were flashing with agitation, and he wanted it gone. "And you, Evie Bennett, are absolutely adorable when you're all riled up."

He kissed her, and the way she melted into him was pure heaven, making him forget, for now, the pain and turmoil he'd been in just a short while ago.

CHAPTER TEN

THE DRIVE TO the Lakeside Camping Resort was a short ten-minute trip from the restaurant—not nearly long enough for Evie to have a conversation about Eric's family with him. She was still blown away by what he'd revealed, and while she'd given him carte blanche to fabricate whatever story he wanted about his background, she knew he'd opted for the truth. There was no way Eric would make up something so devastating. Most importantly, with her hand holding his, she'd literally felt his pain and had seen it etched all over his face after he'd told them he'd had a twin sister who had died so tragically young.

Her heart hurt for him and everything he must have gone through at such a young age— and that still clearly affected him. On the outside, Eric Miller came across as a fun-loving, easygoing guy who seemed to have a charmed life. Or maybe that's just what she wanted to believe since it was easier not to get emotionally attached that way. Which was why she hadn't asked him about his family, or any other personal questions, up to this point. She honestly thought it didn't matter considering he was just a hired boyfriend, but suddenly, his life, his scars and heartaches made a difference to her.

When they arrived at the resort, they drove past the main lodge, where they were scheduled to meet family for a buffet breakfast, and followed the signs to their cabin. Eric parked the car, he grabbed their bags, and they followed the pathway to the cute log structure. They climbed the three stairs to a small porch, and with the key that Evie's mother had given to her, she opened the door and stepped inside.

Since this wasn't her first time at Lakeside, she already knew what the interior of the cabins looked like, but considering she and Eric were essentially going to be living together for the next few days, it suddenly seemed very . . . intimate.

A double-sized bed filled the main room, with an attached bathroom with a walk-in shower and vanity—and there was no overlooking the basket of "goodies" her mother had left propped up against the pillows. From the entrance, you could glimpse the kitchenette around the corner, with a tiny refrigerator, stove, coffeemaker, and table with two chairs. There wasn't a couch or TV. Then again, they weren't there to lie around and spend the weekend watching Netflix. No, Lakeside Camping Resort was all about unplugging and getting in touch with nature.

"I told you the cabin was small," she said, turning to face Eric.

"I didn't expect a penthouse," he joked, though he seemed distracted, and she was pretty sure she knew the cause.

Their dinner conversation was probably still subconsciously on his mind. And since it was a beautiful and cool July evening and dusk was settling in, she decided that she didn't want to spend the rest of the night cooped up in the cabin. Leaving the luggage packed for now, she opened the closet and grabbed an extra quilt-like blanket and tucked it into the crook of her arm, then came back to Eric, who was still standing by the door.

He glanced in confusion at the bed covering she was holding. "What's with the blanket?"

She smiled at him. "I want to take you to a place that you'd never find in the city."

He arched a brow. "Sounds intriguing."

"More like incredibly peaceful." And right now, she was pretty sure he'd welcome the tranquil atmosphere.

As soon as they made their way down the porch and she took a path heading away from the cabin, Eric slipped his hand into her free one, as if it was the most natural thing for him to do. Like they were a real couple. And just like an infatuated schoolgirl with her crush, she felt butterflies fluttering in her stomach.

They continued following the trail, which was lit up by solar path lights that helped lead the way. Before long, they arrived at a small clearing that sloped gently down to the lake. For the most part, they were surrounded by tall pine trees, and with the moon slowly rising, it created a mesmerizing silvery effect on the rippling water. Everything was calm and quiet . . . except for crickets chirping and a distant, occasional hoot of an owl. Nature's harmonica, her grandpa would always say.

Eric stood there for a long moment, taking it all in before he released a deep breath. "Wow. This is a beautiful spot, especially at night."

"It's one of my favorite places to visit when we come here." She was suddenly glad that she'd decided to share it with him. "Sometimes I get lucky, like tonight, and nobody is here."

She opened up the blanket, and Eric helped her spread it out on the grassy knoll. She sat down, adjusting her summer dress accordingly, and patted the spot next to her for him to join her. He didn't hesitate to settle on the blanket beside her, and they both stared out at the lake in companionable silence, enjoying the serene surroundings.

After a while, she turned her head to look at him, though he kept his gaze pinned straight ahead. The moon provided enough illumination for her to see the outline of his strong, handsome profile and those sensual lips she loved having on her own.

She hated to shatter this peaceful moment between them, but she did it anyway. "Eric . . . what happened with your twin sister?" Evie genuinely wanted to know about the sibling he'd lost.

He closed his eyes and groaned. "Evie . . ."

She heard the reluctance in his voice, and before he could refuse her, she added, "Did you really think I wasn't going to ask about her?"

He huffed out a small laugh and turned his head, meeting her gaze. "No, I figured you would. But I was hoping you wouldn't."

Knowing her question wasn't completely unexpected, just unwanted, she gently persisted. "Eric, you could have made up a background and family situation that was ideal and perfect, but you didn't," she said, pointing out the obvious. "You can't just say you had a twin sister who died and not expect me to care enough to want to know what happened. Because I do care." Probably more than was wise.

He gave her a faint but genuine smile. "I know you care, because that's the kind of selfless person you are."

And still, he avoided the topic, so she tried once more. "I imagine it's incredibly painful to talk about, and you've probably discussed it with family more than you care to, but the way you spoke about her at dinner . . . you're clearly still dealing with the pain of losing her." Then again, did a loss like that ever really go away? No, she didn't think so, but Eric's grief still felt fresh and raw, despite the ten plus years that had passed.

"No, I actually haven't talked about it since Trisha died. I mean, there have been rare instances when I've told select people about her and what happened, but never in detail." His jaw hardened ever so slightly. "As for my parents, they both dealt with her death in different, selfish ways, but we never discussed what happened, nor did we grieve Trisha's death together."

Which meant he'd probably suffered alone, and her chest squeezed tightly at the thought. She remained quiet and didn't push for more at this point, leaving it all up to Eric whether or not he decided to share those personal, private details.

Much to her surprise, his stiff shoulders relaxed a fraction, though he kept his gaze focused on the lake, not her. "When Trisha turned fifteen, she started getting frequent infections and bruising and nosebleeds. She was always tired and not feeling well, so of course my mother took her to the doctor to figure out what was wrong. Blood tests showed her platelets were off, and after a bone marrow biopsy, that's when the diagnosis of leukemia came in."

He drew up his knees and rested his arms across them. "From there, she spent a year in treatment and in and out of hospitals. She went through a stem cell transplant, more rounds of chemo and radiation than I can count, and God, she was so strong through it all." He shook his head in wonder as a faint smile touched his lips, then gradually faded. "She lost all her beautiful long hair, and when she decided to shave her head of the few pieces that were left, we did it together so she wouldn't have to do it alone. When she was in the hospital, I spent every day with her, playing games, reading to her, or watching TV. Being twins, she was my best friend and my other half and the thought of losing her scared the shit out of me."

He scrubbed a hand along his jaw and finally glanced at Evie, his eyes so somber it made her want to cry past the huge lump gathering in her throat. "We had a few months of believing she was in remission . . . but the leukemia came back, faster and stronger than before. She agreed to more chemo and radiation . . . and God, seeing how sick and how much pain she was in after her treatments, it nearly killed me, and I kept thinking, why couldn't I have been the one to get the cancer instead of my sister? I would have gladly traded places with her. I would have fucking died for her."

His voice sounded like it had been scraped across gravel, and Evie leaned closer to him, looping her arm through his. Since she knew there were no words to ease his anguish, she cuddled up to his side just to be near him, so he knew he wasn't alone emotionally.

He exhaled a ragged breath. "Then came the words *she's terminal,* and I remember screaming at my parents that it couldn't be true. That Trisha did everything to kick cancer's ass and she was going to fucking make it . . . except she didn't." He rubbed his fingers across his eyes, and the rawness of his voice told Evie he was wiping away tears. "I held her hand when she drew her last breath and passed away, and a huge part of me died that day right along with her. There's a part inside of me that's been hollow ever since."

His story ripped at Evie's insides like nothing ever had, and she couldn't contain the sob that escaped her throat or the tears that fell from the corners of her eyes. "I'm so sorry," she whispered through her own emotions.

He turned his head and gently, sweetly kissed her temple. "I know," he murmured. "Me, too."

Wrapping one arm around her, he lay back on the blanket, bringing her down with him so that she was snuggled against his chest and her head rested on his shoulder. His fingers filtered through her hair, playing with the strands, while she slid an arm around his midsection, holding him tight, wishing there were more words to take away his grief. *I'm sorry* just didn't seem adequate enough.

He stared up at the stars twinkling in the clear night sky. "Before Trisha passed away, we had the best parents, family, and childhood any kid could ask for. But after she died, nothing was the same. Not that I expected it to be, obviously, but I thought I'd at least be able to count on my parents to be there for me. I was only sixteen at the time, still in high school, and I *needed* them to be there for me."

He shook his head sadly, and Evie just let him talk.

"My parents wouldn't discuss her death. They shut down emotionally. My father . . . he spent more time at work than at home, probably because my mother withdrew from everyone and fell into a deep depression, and for the next two years, it was like living in this bleak, gloomy atmosphere where I kept my own pain bottled up inside. When I finally graduated from high school, my parents divorced and I moved into a dorm at San Diego State University instead of living at home. I just couldn't be in that environment anymore."

God, he'd had everything snatched away from him so quickly. His sister. His parents. Normal teenager years. It sounded as though he'd gone from a stable, secure childhood to a shattered one that couldn't be put back together. "Living in a dorm was probably for the best," she said.

"It was," he agreed, placing his hand over hers that was resting on his chest. "I was surrounded by friends and distracted, but looking back, I really should have seen a therapist," he said with a hoarse laugh. "I felt so guilty that I was the one to live and my sister was the one to die. It was so fucking unfair, and that thought really messed with my head because I had no one to talk to about it."

"Survivor's guilt," she murmured, certain that's what he'd gone through.

He breathed deep, and she felt the rise and fall of his chest beneath her palm. "Yes, I know that now, though I'd like to think that I've come to terms with the fact that I can't change what happened or who it happened to."

"They say that it's always the hardest on the ones left behind when someone dies," she said softly.

"So true," he agreed. "Watching someone die like that and feeling so helpless and having your heart torn into a million different pieces . . . It's something I never want to put anyone through, and I swore I never would."

She lifted her head from his shoulder so she could see his face, confused by his statement. "How so?"

A wry smile barely touched his lips, but she saw it in the moonlight and it made her stomach twist uncomfortably. "Trish and I were fraternal twins. We shared the same genetic profile. I've read articles and there is a risk that I could develop cancer, too."

Shock rippled through her. She'd only known Eric a short while, but that possibility wasn't something she even wanted to consider. "You can't live your life thinking like that."

He shrugged, and she could see the resignation in his eyes as he looked into hers. "I already have, Evie. It's why I've never had a long-term relationship."

She gaped at him in disbelief. "Ever?"

"*Ever*," he stated adamantly.

She shook her head incredulously. "How is that even possible at your age?"

"It's possible because of everything I just told you," he said, as if it were that simple. And for him, it probably was that straightforward. "I'm not going to put some woman through that possibility, then end up breaking her heart. It's not fair to her. I'm not going to build a family with someone and chance leaving a wife without a husband and kids without a father. It's just easier to keep things light and casual."

His rationale seemed so extreme . . . but then again, it made sense, too, considering his traumatic past. "Eric, you deserve to be happy, just like anyone else." Despite the risks he faced.

He lifted his hand and brushed back the hair that had fallen forward and around her face as she glanced down at him. "I am happy."

Maybe superficially, she thought, but he was living only half of what should have been a whole, fulfilled life. And the fact that he'd likely never experience a true, deep sense of joy and someone to share it with because of his fears wrecked her own heart a little bit.

She realized there was nothing else she could say to make him change his mind, and because she was desperate to make him feel more than just pain, she lowered her head and kissed him. As soon as her mouth brushed across his, he groaned deep in his throat and his hand tangled in her hair, tight and urgent, as he crushed his lips against hers.

They parted beneath the onslaught of his silent demand, and she gave herself openly and generously, and he took greedily, the sweep of his tongue claiming every inch of her mouth. She tasted his raw, vulnerable emotion, his grief, his sorrow . . . which gradually gave way to heat, desire, and the bright burn of passion.

With a low, possessive growl, he rolled her beneath him on the blanket, so his firm body half covered hers and she felt the hard length of his erection digging against her hip. He nudged his knee between hers, and her legs spread shamelessly for him, while the hand still wrapped in her hair tugged on her scalp to tip her head back, giving him better, deeper access to her mouth. The urgency in him was wild and reckless, his lips unyielding against hers, as if imprinting the taste of her in his mind would obliterate everything else he'd just shared with her.

She curled her fingers into his shirt and let him have free rein, and when his other hand pushed beneath the hem of her dress and squeezed her upper thigh, there was no holding back the mewling sound of need that reverberated through her. His hot palm skimmed higher, his thumb brushing along the damp panel of cotton covering her sex, then gliding up to her clit. He pressed and rubbed her through the increasingly wetter fabric, making her ache so damn good. Her hips bucked of their own accord against the hand between her legs, trying to increase the pressure, the friction . . . anything to give her body the release it craved.

He continued kissing her as his fingers moved away, and she whimpered against his lips at the loss of his touch, pulled tighter on his shirt to draw him closer, but she didn't have to worry, because seconds later he was sliding his hand into her panties, touching her skin on skin, his long fingers tunneling right into all the wetness he'd created, before two of them plunged deep into her core.

Shocked by the sudden, unexpected fullness, she tore her lips from his and gasped for breath, her entire body tensing, then quivering as the pads of those two fingers rubbed a spot that had her shaking and her clit pulsing. She buried her face in his neck, panting, so close to orgasming that it was embarrassing. She *never* came this fast.

He didn't let her hide. He gently pulled her head back, a sinful, knowing smile seducing her even more. He looked into her eyes, his so dark and hungry, and somewhere in the back of her mind, she realized that she'd never had a man look at her like that before ... with such undeniable want and unbridled lust.

"Let me watch you take your pleasure so I can forget everything else," he murmured, pumping his fingers out, then back in again. His thumb joined in on the action, swirling around that hard, sensitive nub of flesh, teasing her.

She bit her bottom lip to hold in a blissful moan and caught a glimpse of the dark night sky studded with stars above Eric, reminding her exactly where they were. "Eric ... we're out in the open," she reminded him.

"So?" he said in a low, sex-infused voice, undeterred by her concern, so much so that he continued to fuck her with his fingers, slowly, deeply. "I have my hand beneath your skirt, but we're both fully clothed, so no indecent exposure happening here. Besides, nobody is around except the crickets and the owl."

He lowered his head and swiped his tongue along her bottom lip, the same way his thumb danced across her needy clit. "Give me your orgasm, baby," he ordered gruffly. "I want to feel you tighten and pulse against my fingers so I can imagine how you'd feel around my dick as I'm fucking you and making you come so hard that I'm the only thing you can think of as you bask in all that decadent pleasure."

His skillful, assertive fingers brought her to the brink, but his dirty talk sent her over the edge. She stared helplessly into his hot and avid gaze, her face flushing and her lips parting to release the soft cry she knew was coming as she fell headlong into the throes of an orgasm so all-consuming she lost all sense of time and place.

Eric's mouth crashed down on hers, catching the scream before it fully formed and turning it into a long, lingering moan against his lips. Her body quaked, and when he finally, gradually withdrew his fingers, she mourned the loss. Better yet, she wanted to feel *him* pushing deep inside her, again and again.

He smoothed her dress back down to her knees and drew her into his arms, holding her close with her head on his chest and his lips near her ear. "Jesus Christ, that was so fucking hot," he growled.

She laughed, but before she could give him all the credit or reach down and unfasten his pants so she could return the favor and get her hands on his rock-hard erection, the sound of someone nearby clearing their throat stopped her from following through on that thought.

She stiffened, mortification settling over her. She squeezed her eyes shut against his chest and didn't move, but Eric lifted his head and glanced around.

"Oh . . . Hey . . . Hi, Mr. and Mrs. Bennett," Eric said amicably, as if he hadn't just had his hand between their daughter's legs, giving her the best orgasm of her life. "Beautiful night out, isn't it?"

"It is," Gene agreed from a distance not too far away, probably closer to the lake. "Lauren and I had the same idea as you two, but clearly you kids are smarter and quicker than we are."

Evie cringed. *Oh my God, no.* She untangled herself from Eric's arms and stood up. "We're leaving, because I'm not sticking around to watch my parents make out."

Her father chuckled, the devilish sound telling her that they'd indeed come to this spot for that very reason. "Keep the sex down in the cabin tonight. Don't want someone to call the ranger to report loud noises, if you know what I mean."

Eric snickered as they folded the blanket together.

Her mother decided to add her two cents to the conversation. "If she's not moaning and making noises, how will Eric know he's hitting all her pleasure zones?"

Evie prayed for the ground to open up and swallow her whole.

With a playful sparkle in his eyes, Eric leaned close and whispered, "I think I managed okay, don't you?"

She narrowed her gaze at him. "Don't you start, too. It'll just encourage them!"

"Trust me," her father went on, unaware of Eric and Evie's side conversation. "Eric seems like a smart guy who can figure it out. Besides, most of us don't need a map, dear."

"Well, you don't, anyway." Her mother giggled.

Blanket folded, Evie called out to her parents. "Good night. See you in the morning." And before they could see or hear anything between her parents that would scar Evie for life, she power-walked back to the cabin, with Eric keeping pace beside her, chuckling beneath his breath.

CHAPTER ELEVEN

Eric stood beneath the shower spray in the incredibly tiny stall, where even turning around with his wide shoulders was a bit tricky. When he and Evie had arrived back at the cabin after their run-in with her parents, he'd decided that he needed a few minutes to himself to refresh and reboot, so to speak. Especially after the emotional conversation he'd had with Evie about his sister . . . followed by touching Evie and watching her come apart for him.

He'd gone from one extreme . . . experiencing that gut punch of grief when he thought about his sister and what she'd gone through, to being intimate with a sweet, guileless woman who made him feel things he had no business allowing to infiltrate his heart. Not even a little bit.

He couldn't say that he'd been surprised when she'd asked about Trisha . . . but he'd been floored that she'd actually cried over his sister. A girl she'd never known. All because *he'd* been hurting, and she'd felt his pain. Jesus, even his own mother hadn't shown *him* that kind of emotion, or acknowledged his grief.

He hadn't wanted to tell Evie about Trisha and his family, but now that he had, he couldn't say he regretted sharing his past. As he scrubbed the shampoo through his hair, he admitted that he felt a little lighter inside, like a small burden had been lifted . . . though their conversation didn't change how he viewed relationships and forever commitments. He'd meant what he'd said to Evie about keeping his relationships casual, and his reasons for doing so. He was too much of a risk factor, and he refused to put any woman through the same agony and heartbreak he'd lived through with Trisha.

He finished rinsing the soap from his body, turned off the water, and stepped out of the shower. Grabbing a towel, he rubbed it through his wet hair, dried off the best he could . . . and realized that he'd left the sleep shorts he'd intended to wear to bed tonight in his bag in the other room. No big deal. He'd just wrap the towel around his waist and go grab them really quick.

As soon as he stepped out of the bathroom, he came to an abrupt halt, his breath lodging in his throat at the sight of Evie sitting on the edge of the bed a few feet away from him, wearing a tempting dark pink nightie that was hot as fuck. Thin, miniscule straps held up the sexy little number, while pink, see-through lace molded to her lush breasts and sheer material floated down to her thighs.

His cock stirred and stiffened against the scratchy terry material around his waist as he lifted his gaze back to hers. "I . . . uh . . . Is that what you always sleep in?"

She laughed softly, sensually. "No. I bought it a few days ago . . . just in case."

Her insinuation was clear. She wanted to have sex with him. After what they'd just done down by the lake, he should have been all over her and the invitation she was issuing, but this was Evie, not some random fuck buddy of his. She knew he didn't do long-term relationships; he'd made that clear earlier. He had strict rules, yet he'd bet all his money in the bank that she was the kind of woman who probably didn't have much experience in random flings, and yet that's all this could be.

She was the last person he'd ever want to

hurt, because he legitimately cared about her. More than he'd ever thought possible. How the fuck had that even happened?

"Evie . . . I'm not sure this is such a good idea."

She stood up and closed the distance between them, and his traitorous gaze dipped down to the nipples poking through the pink lace, taunting him with what he couldn't have. When she stopped about a foot away from him, he dragged his gaze back up to her beautiful face, framed by all that gorgeous, thick brown hair his hands were itching to feel wrapped tight around his fingers again.

"Here's the deal," she said, and he didn't miss the slight vulnerable note to her voice. "I'm not asking you for more than you're willing to give. And right now, if it's just sex, then I want it with you. You can't touch me like you did down by the lake and not expect me to want more." She swallowed hard. "Unless . . . you're not interested?"

Shock jolted through him. Jesus, how could she think that after what had happened between them? That he'd pleasured her out of, what, obligation on his part as her pretend boyfriend? Fuck no. He was *trying* to do the right thing, but

172

his resolve was quickly dwindling. God, he was such a dick for wanting her so much . . . and an even bigger asshole for being greedy and taking what she was offering when he knew he could only give her this weekend.

Taking her hand, he flattened her palm on his bare, damp chest, nearly groaning at the soft, cool contact of her skin on his hot flesh. Desire flared in her eyes as he gradually guided her hand down his body, letting her feel the way his abs tightened at her touch and how his breathing deepened the closer she drifted to his stiff, straining erection.

He tucked her fingers into the knot keeping the towel in place around his hips and gave her a daring smile. "Why don't you take off my towel and find out for yourself just how *interested* I am."

Her tongue skimmed along her bottom lip, and Jesus Christ, his dick pulsed, craving the feel of her soft mouth wrapped around his shaft as she sucked the length deep into her throat. More blood rushed to his groin, stretching his cock tight. If she didn't follow through, he was going to have to take another shower, this one ice cold, or else he'd never sleep tonight.

"So, what's it going to be, baby?" he murmured seductively as he toyed with the thin strap of her nightie, so damn tempted to push it off her shoulder so he could see her bare breasts. "Towel . . . or no towel?"

She gave him a brazen smile and tugged on the knot, releasing the swath of terry material, which promptly fell to the floor at his feet, leaving him completely naked. "No towel," she whispered, and trailed her fingers lower, until they curled around his thick shaft and she stroked him in her fist.

With a guttural groan, he leaned against the wall next to the bathroom, and she stepped closer. She dipped her head, placing a warm, damp kiss on his collarbone, then continued stringing more of them across his chest and along his taut stomach. She settled on her knees in front of him, still holding his dick nice and snug in her hand, and he glanced down, watching as her pretty pink lips parted over the head of his cock, then slid all the way down to the base before she hollowed her cheeks and sucked her way back up to the tip.

His entire body shuddered with pleasure and need. Instinctively, he buried his hands in her hair, tipped his head back against the wall, and selfishly enjoyed the wet, suctioning heat of her mouth working the length of his dick, loving the way she moaned her own appreciation around his cock, how she swiped her tongue over the weeping slit before going back for more.

He hadn't expected her to go down on him, but fuck . . . for as amazing as her mouth felt, there was no way he was coming down her throat before he'd even had the chance to experience the silken heat of her pussy around his shaft. He tugged her back up to her feet and easily maneuvered her so that their positions were switched and she now had her back up against the wall.

She stared at him in surprise through dark, hazy blue eyes. Her face was flushed with desire, her lips swollen from sucking his dick, and as he held her gaze, he slipped his fingers beneath both straps of her lingerie and pulled them down her arms until the entire nightie drifted its way down to her feet and her breasts were bared to his gaze.

He didn't hesitate to put his hands on them, squeezing the soft flesh and lightly pinching her stiff nipples until she whimpered and squirmed. Wanting to enjoy every inch of her, he dipped his head and kissed her neck, nuzzling his way down her throat. Her hands shot up, twisting in his hair, tugging on the strands . . . not to pull him away but to hold him closer . . . *as if he was going anywhere.*

By the time he reached her full, generous tits, his mouth was watering for a taste, and he didn't deny himself. He latched on to a nipple, sucking gently, laving his tongue over and around the bead of flesh before scraping his teeth across the tip, while his other hand worked the opposite breast, pinching, teasing, and rolling the nipple between his fingers.

The softest, sexiest sounds fell from her lips, and she arched her back against the wall as he kissed his way down her stomach, his hands tracing the indentation of her waist and the lush curves of her hips. He knelt in front of her, his eyes on the sweet, pink lace panties she wore that looked like sexy booty shorts . . . instead of the soft, white cotton he'd expected. Not that he was complaining.

He sat back on his heels and looked up at her flushed, aroused face with a smile. "Face the wall for a sec," he ordered gently, because there was something specific he was dying to see and put his hands on.

He saw the reluctance in her eyes and refused to let modesty get in the way of his request. "Don't go all shy on me now, baby. I want to see your perfect ass covered in this pretty lace you wore just for me."

She did as he asked, resting her arms on the wall with her feet slightly apart as her back curved just enough to jut her hips out in a perfect fucking position. *Jesus*, between the provocative angle of her bottom and her hair spilling down her bare back and that delicate lace riding high on her ass cheeks, it was all he could do not to stand back up and take her from behind right then and there.

His cock throbbed, and he ignored the ache for now as he smoothed his palms up the backs of her thighs, dipped his thumbs between her legs, and followed the crease of her ass all the way up to the base of her spine. She moaned sensually as he slid his fingers inside the elastic band of her panties and slowly, gradually peeled them down her legs, placing hot, open-mouthed kisses on the skin he exposed, until the underwear finally dropped to the floor to join the other half of her outfit.

From where he was kneeling, he could see how wet and swollen her pussy already was, and that's what he wanted next. "Turn around," he ordered, and this time, there was zero delay on her part as she faced him again.

Sliding a hand between her thighs and feeling her slick heat coat his fingers, he tipped his head back so he was looking into her eyes, which were glazed with the same lust surging through his veins. He deliberately licked his lips and gave her a wicked, dirty grin. "You know what I want, don't you?"

Her lashes fell half-mast, and she smiled almost coquettishly, turning into a vixen right before his eyes. "Yes, I think I might have an idea."

Did she now, he thought in amusement. "Are you going to let me have it?" he asked huskily as he glided his thumb through her pillowy flesh. "Are you going to let me eat this sweet, luscious pussy?"

She nodded eagerly. "Yes, please," she breathed.

He moved closer, pressing his free hand against Evie's hip to steady her for what he was about to do. "Put your other leg over my shoulder, sweetheart. I want you nice and open for me."

She complied, exposing herself to him, and he leaned forward, burying his face between her legs and feasting on her pussy. She gasped in shock, her hands gripping his shoulders, her nails biting into his skin as his tongue explored and stroked and lashed her clit until she was panting, trembling, and rocking her hips against his mouth in an attempt to chase her building orgasm.

Needy, sultry, desperate sounds fell from her lips, the same kind of noises she'd made down by the lake before she'd splintered apart, and as cruel as it might be for her, he stopped before her climax reached its peak and stood back up.

"Nooo," she whimpered, shaking her head wildly in disappointment.

"That orgasm fucking belongs to *me*," he said gruffly, uncaring that he probably sounded like a possessive asshole as he grabbed the backs of Evie's thighs and lifted her high enough that she instinctively wrapped her legs around his hips. He walked with her to the bed, which was only a few steps away. "You're going to come when I'm as deep as I can get inside of you so I can feel your pussy tightening and squeezing my cock, milking everything out of me."

His filthy words made her duck her head

against his neck and moan in agreement.

Depositing her on the mattress, he pushed her down and came so goddamn close to thrusting inside her bareback until he remembered that he needed a condom. Jesus Christ, he *never* had sex without protection. Ever. That's what this woman did to him . . . made him forget all thought, logic, and the rules he'd spent his adult life living by.

The basket of stuff her mother had left for them was on the nightstand within reaching distance, and remembering seeing a twelve pack of rubbers tucked in with all the other interesting items, he fished it out, almost laughing when he read the *Ultra Ribbed For Her Pleasure* slogan stamped across the front of the box, but damn if he wasn't grateful to Lauren for providing what he'd stupidly forgotten to bring with him.

He retrieved a foil wrapper, tore it open, and rolled the condom on in record speed before coming back down on top of her. Her legs were spread wide to accommodate his hips, and the head of his cock glided through her slick heat and zeroed in on her center. He pushed in a few inches and paused.

Her eyes flared with panic. "Don't you *dare*

stop," she said, grabbing *his* ass to keep him in place.

He laughed at what a spitfire she'd suddenly become. "Not gonna happen, baby," he assured her. Not when he was already at the gates of heaven. "Hook your legs around my waist, as high as you can get."

She obeyed, the position tilting her hips up so he had the best leverage possible, because this was *not* going to be a slow, leisurely screw. It was going to be hard and fast and maybe even uncivilized since that's what his body was clamoring for.

"Fucking perfect," he muttered, and drove the rest of the way into her, planting himself to the hilt in one swift, deep plunge.

She sucked in a startled breath, then a blissful sound of pleasure filled his ears as she strained beneath him, and that's all he needed to hear and feel to know she could take what he was about to deliver. He slid his hands into her hair, holding her head in place as his mouth came down hungrily over hers as she matched his wild, uncontrolled rhythm, her hips lifting and undulating to meet his driving thrusts.

He'd left her on the verge of climax just minutes ago, and it didn't take long for her to make that climb to the precipice again. She moaned against his lips, and as soon as he felt the beginning of those fluttering sensations he'd experienced around his fingers earlier, he tore his mouth from hers so he could watch her fall over the edge . . . and take him with her this time.

Her blue eyes glazed over with ecstasy, and she bite her bottom lip to hold back her cry of pleasure as her inner muscles rippled around his shaft, throbbing and releasing, until the hot, slick pressure became more than he could resist. He grunted out her name as her body continued to quiver and pulse, coaxing every drop of come right out of him in a mind-numbing release.

With one last deep thrust because she felt so fucking good, he collapsed on top of her, careful not to crush her with his weight. She relaxed beneath him, and as boneless as her, Eric didn't want to move. Didn't want to break their connection when nothing had ever felt so perfectly right. That intimate thought sent a jolt of panic through him because he never lingered inside a woman after fucking her. That was just asking for all sorts of emotional trouble.

Ignoring the dull pang in the vicinity of his chest, he lifted himself up and eased out of her sated body, and the way she smiled up at him so dreamily, so affectionately, fucking eviscerated him inside because she made him ache for that kind of tenderness in his life on a regular basis. Which wasn't going to happen.

"I'll be right back," he murmured, and disappeared into the bathroom.

He took care of the condom, then braced his hands on the sink and scowled at his reflection in the mirror. "It's just sex," he muttered to himself. "It's just sex. It's just *fucking* sex."

He didn't feel any better, because no matter how many times he said the words, he didn't quite believe them.

CHAPTER TWELVE

EVIE WOKE TO a deliciously hot, hard, distinctly male body pressing hers into the mattress, and she smiled into her pillow, because she was pretty damn sure she was about to get lucky with a hot, toe-curling round of morning sex. Her favorite kind.

She'd always been a stomach sleeper, and she'd drifted off naked, so it was easy enough for Eric to slid up over her from behind, nudge her legs apart with his knees, and settle his hips between her now spread thighs. The head of his shaft found her entrance, teasing her with a prodding pressure that promised to fill her with the hard length of his cock. Eventually.

She hugged her pillow a little tighter. "Good morning," she murmured, letting him know that she was awake and aware and totally on board with his idea. Even after using up three condoms during the course of the night, she was far from done enjoying this sexy part of her weekend with Eric . . . so long as she kept the physical separated from the emotional. So far, so good . . . or so she kept telling herself. Maybe, eventually, she'd believe it.

"Mmm." He pushed her hair to one side, nuzzled her neck for a few seconds, then gently bit the curve of her shoulder, causing a zing of pleasure to race all the way down to her pussy. "It's about to be a fucking *fantastic* morning, sweetheart."

The growl in his voice made her sensitive nipples pucker against the sheets. "Yeah?" she taunted playfully.

"Oh, yeah," he echoed huskily, tossing aside her pillow before he grabbed her hands and stretched them a few inches above her head.

Anticipation hummed through her at the dominant position. Who knew she liked a man to be so confident and assertive in bed? All her past lovers were tame in comparison to Eric. "So far, you're all talk and no real action," she teased.

"Is that right?" he drawled in her ear, his voice taking on an indecent edge.

"Mm-hmm." She brazenly shimmied her ass against his hips, making him groan as his dick lodged a little deeper. "Is this all you got, Mr.

Miller? Pinning me down and teasing me with two inches of your cock?"

An abrupt gust of laughter escaped him. "God damn, you're sassy in the morning." His mouth brushed her ear again, followed by his tongue rimming the outer shell. "I like it when you're feisty."

"It's called put up or shut up, mister," she challenged shamelessly.

"I'm all about putting up, baby." Holding both of her wrists in one hand, he reached down with the other and glided the head of his condom-covered cock through her folds, gathering the wetness there before returning to the entry to her body and pushing excruciatingly slowly inside her.

His chest pressed her breasts to the bed, and his hips deliberately held hers firmly down to the mattress so she had no wiggle room and he was in complete control of how his cock gradually stretched its way inside her.

She couldn't hold back the groan that rumbled up from her throat. His unhurried pace was pure, delicious, decadent torture. Last night had been all about fast, dirty, hot sex. When Eric had returned from the bathroom after their first time, she'd noticed a change in him, and the second and third round of fucking had been edgy, reckless, and far from gentle or sweet, like maybe he was trying to keep things purely physical, which she completely understood and appreciated considering they both knew this thing between them was just a weekend affair.

Last night, she'd promised him she'd only take what he was willing to give, and for him, that was offering her the best sex she'd ever had and would probably never experience again. And while he made it increasingly difficult not to want more than just a short-term tryst, she wasn't going to ruin their time together by making demands or expecting him to change who he was, who he'd been since his sister's death. He'd been honest with her about not being a forever kind of guy, and she had to respect that, no matter how difficult she already knew that was going to be in the end.

He moved inside her from behind, with-drawing slowly and pushing back in with equal languor, her ass tight against his hips as he pumped into her, building the tension inside of her yet not providing enough friction against her clit to get her where she needed to go. She would have used her own fingers to get herself off if he hadn't had them in lockdown above her head.

"Stop teasing me," she moaned desperately, hating that she still couldn't move, that he had all the power and she was helpless to just surrender to him.

"What would you like, baby?" he asked, much too sweetly as he scraped his teeth up the side of her neck, eliciting a rush of wet heat between her thighs that slickened the length of his cock as he pulled out to the tip. "Tell me what you need, and *maybe* I'll let you have it."

"I need to come while you're fucking me like this." She was beyond caring that she was pleading and panting. "Please."

"That can definitely be arranged." She heard the satisfied smile in his voice as he shifted slightly, then his free hand moved between her hips and the mattress.

She was expecting his fingers to work their magic, but instead felt something hard and cool press against her clit. Before she could comprehend what it was, she heard the click of a switch, and the mini vibrator Evie had seen in the basket of sex aids her mother had given them came to life with a low, steady hum against that needy, hard knot of flesh.

She gasped in shock, her entire body instantly lighting up as though she'd stuck her finger into an electrical socket. Her stomach tumbled, her thighs shook, and behind her, Eric chuckled sinfully in her ear.

She gathered the sheets in her fists, trying desperately to twist beneath him, to rub against the device that felt like a dozen tongues flicking at her clit. "Eric . . . *please* let me move."

"Mmm." He buried his face in her hair and, much to her relief, released her hands. "You beg so prettily, so yes, you can move." His lower body eased up slightly on hers, allowing her to grind down on the vibe, but his thick erection wasn't nearly as deep as she needed it to be.

"It's not enough," she moaned, wondering when she'd become so wanton and demanding.

"What do you want now?" he asked, his voice rough with amusement.

She huffed out a frustrated breath because he already knew the answer to his question. He was just forcing her to say the dirty words out loud. "I want you to fuck me. Hard. Deep."

"Greedy girl." The husky sound of his voice shot straight to her core. "How about you fuck yourself on my cock and take whatever you want, however you need?"

He gave her just enough room to push back and impale herself on his shaft while riding the vibrating toy he held firmly against her clit. She undulated her hips, rocking back and forth, taking him again and again until the friction of his cock, combined with the relentless humming between her legs, had her entire body shaking with the strength of her release.

The force of it was so intense her lips parted to release a scream of pleasure, only to feel Eric's big hand cover her mouth to muffle what would have alerted anyone in the nearby vicinity what they were doing inside the cabin. In her ear, he grunted and groaned and swore as he slammed into her from behind, driving impossibly deeper as he came right along with her.

As far as mornings went, it was one of the best ones she'd had in a long time.

ERIC TOOK A shower first, changed into a T-shirt and swim trunks since they had the canoe race today, and waited for Evie to finish up in the bathroom before they headed to the lodge for breakfast, where he'd meet the rest of her family that had come to the reunion.

A few minutes later, she came out in a tank top and shorts, though he could see that she was wearing a one-piece bathing suit beneath. She had on only minimal makeup, and he liked her fresh-faced and natural, especially since her cheeks were still pink and flushed from this morning's satisfying round of sex.

She slid her feet into a pair of flip-flops, slipped an elastic band around her wrist to put up her hair later for the canoe race, and smiled at him. "Ready to go before my mother comes banging on our door?"

"Give me a minute." He walked up to her, and she let out a startled sound as he buried his fingers in her hair and brought her lips to his and kissed her deeply, passionately.

She tasted like mint and so warm and addicting he wondered how he was going to get enough of her over the next two days. While she gripped the front of his shirt to keep herself steady as she melted into him, he took the next two minutes to devour her mouth—his lips, tongue, and teeth, along with his fingers deliberately disheveling her hair, all joining in to make sure she looked completely and utterly ravished.

By the time he ended the kiss and took in

the arousal that painted her cheeks pink and the blissful look in her blue eyes, he was pleased with his accomplishment. "There. *Now* we're ready. You might not look freshly fucked, but there is no denying I just kissed the hell out of you. Your lips are red and a little swollen, and your hair is just tousled enough that it'll be crystal clear to Raquel and Graham, or anyone else who looks at you, that I find you absolutely irresistible." Which was the truth.

She lifted her hand to fix the strands he'd deliberately mussed up, and he grabbed her wrist to stop her, shaking his head. "Leave your hair alone and own it, Evie, because you're a beautiful, desirable woman and you need to embrace that." If Eric did anything for her this weekend, he wanted to build her confidence after the dickheads she'd dated had destroyed it.

So another man can enjoy your efforts? his mind taunted him. Yeah, he didn't like the thought of another guy touching her or kissing her or fucking her . . . and that certainly was a new and foreign feeling for him.

"Isn't that what you hired me for?" he asked, reminding her as much as himself of his reasons for being here. "To make sure everyone believes that you have a boyfriend who can't keep his hands off you?"

She gave him a half smile. "You do your job almost too well. In fact, you're not too bad at this whole boyfriend thing, considering you've never had a girlfriend."

"You're *my* first girlfriend experience." He winked at her, meaning it purely as part of the whole boyfriend experience gig, but he was beginning to realize that the feelings swirling inside him weren't part of the act. And that scared the crap out of him. More than he cared to admit.

Hand in hand, they headed up to the main lodge for the breakfast buffet, and when they arrived, they were directed to a room that had been reserved for the family reunion for the weekend. They were greeted by the savory scent of eggs, bacon, and coffee, and his stomach growled accordingly.

The first person to greet them, of course, was Evie's mother, Lauren, who came up to her daughter and patted her cheeks. "Look at you! You're glowing this morning," she said, pretty much insinuating that sex or a few orgasms were the reason for Evie's lustrous complexion, which Eric supposed they were.

"And so are you, Mom," she deadpanned,

and Eric bit back the smile at the small thread of sarcasm in Evie's voice. Yeah, definitely feisty this morning.

Lauren blinked at her in surprise, then smiled. "Why, I suppose I am," she admitted unabashedly. "Morning sex is the best way to start the day, am I right?"

"Couldn't agree more," Eric chimed in, truly enjoying Lauren's refreshing personality, even if she did embarrass Evie, which he found adorable. "Followed by a well-balanced breakfast, of course, to replace all the calories that were burned." He rubbed his stomach.

Beside him, Evie groaned beneath her breath.

"That's true." Lauren nodded in agreement. "You've got a canoe race to attend, and you're going to need to build that energy and stamina back up if you two want to win."

He grinned at Evie's mom. "Yes, ma'am. Energy and stamina. Got it."

Lauren shifted her gaze back to Evie, her expression suddenly serious. "Honey, if you haven't already figured it out, this one's a keeper. Not nearly as uptight as you-know-who," she added out of the side of her mouth.

Eric was still holding Evie's hand, and he

felt her tense as she surreptitiously glanced around the room, obviously looking for Graham and Raquel, the two people she probably dreaded seeing the most.

"Are they here yet?" The barest hint of anxiety touched her voice.

"They checked in last night but I haven't seen them for breakfast yet," her mother said. "But we still have another forty minutes before they clear the buffet. Why don't you introduce Eric around real quick so everyone knows who he is, and then get something to eat."

Evie nodded and directed him toward her dad, who was drinking a cup of coffee and standing with a small group of people close to his own age. As soon as Gene saw Evie, his eyes lit up, happy to have his daughter near for the weekend, and he drew her close to his side in a warm, affectionate hug.

"Morning, Dad," she said, smiling at her father.

"Hey, baby girl." He kissed her temple and shifted his gaze over her head to Eric. "Son," he added with a welcoming, l-like-you kind of nod.

"Morning, sir," he replied.

Evie started in on the introductions, giving him the boyfriend label he'd been hired to play.

There was a whirlwind of aunts and uncles and cousins and their kids, all on Evie's father's side of the family, not that he was going to remember anyone's name, so he just nodded and smiled. Evie made the rounds with obligatory hugs, and he followed right behind her with handshakes and *it's a pleasure to meet you.*

Just when he thought they were done and they were going to head toward the buffet because he was freaking starved, an older gentleman walked into the room, and the transformation on Evie's face was a beautiful thing to behold—a huge smile, happiness, and unconditional love all wrapped up in an elated expression.

"Grandpa!" she called out, and raced toward the man from across the room, nearly crashing into him with the force of the hug she wrapped around him. "Oh my God. I've missed you so much!"

The older man laughed as he embraced her in return, the love between them evident. "I've missed you, too." He released her and smiled. "And I know you told me the news over the phone, but I can't tell you how proud I am of your nomination for the Humanitarian Award. I knew you would do amazing things in San

Diego."

"Thanks to you," she said, her voice grateful, reminding Eric of how her grandfather had given her the money to start her business. "You know I couldn't have done it without your help."

He made a dismissive gesture with his hand, as if it was nothing, and turned toward Eric. Her grandfather gave him a shrewd once-over, clearly checking to make sure he was good enough for his granddaughter. "And you must be Eric," he said.

He assumed that Evie had told her grandfather about him . . . well, the *ex*-Eric anyway. "Yes, sir. It's a pleasure to finally meet you. Evie speaks very highly of you. It's clear she adores you."

Her grandfather chucked Evie gently beneath the chin, his eyes crinkling at the corners as he smiled. "I feel the same way about her." He glanced over to the coffee station. "I need a double shot of caffeine if I'm going to be at the top of my game for everything Lauren has planned today. I'll talk to you two more later."

"Sounds good," Eric said, thinking they'd follow Evie's grandfather in the same direction for food and drink before his stomach went on strike from being so damn hungry.

"Sissy!"

The word was yelled from somewhere behind Eric, and he glanced over his shoulder just in time to see a good-looking guy, who was wearing pastel plaid shorts and a neon pink tank top, heading straight toward Evie. The dark-haired giant picked her up in his arms and spun her around, while she gave him a mock insufferable look that made Eric curious to find out who the younger man was.

Finally, the grinning guy set her back down on her feet and Evie scowled at him. "You know how much I hate it when you call me Sissy."

"Of course I do," he replied with an unrepentant laugh. "You're my sister, and you know Sissy has always been my nickname for you. Why would that change now?"

"Because we're adults?" she suggested, just as her brother—her *gay* brother, if Eric remembered correctly—turned his striking blue eyes Eric's way.

The other man was not discreet about checking out Eric, and by the time he was done with his perusal, he was smirking at Evie. "I see you brought me some hot eye candy for the weekend." Then he thrust his hand out toward Eric. "I'm Garrett, by the way. The fashionable one in the family."

"Eric. Evie's boyfriend," he said, introducing himself. Garrett had a firm handshake and a great sense of humor, as far as Eric could tell.

Her brother gave him another appreciative once-over. "Damn, you really scored with this one, Sissy."

Evie rolled her eyes. "Take your eyes off the merchandise, Garrett. I promise you, he doesn't play for the same team, and where is Aaron, by the way?" she asked, leading Eric to believe Aaron was her brother's boyfriend.

"He'll be here in a few minutes." Garrett exhaled an impatient sigh. "He couldn't decide on whether to wear his rainbow swim trunks today or the ones with the dolphins on them."

Evie pressed a hand to her chest, feigning distress. "Oh, the dilemma."

"Right?" Garrett responded dramatically. "I told him he shouldn't wear either because, *hello*, we'll clash, but you know how stubborn he can be."

Evie laughed. "No more than you, dear brother."

"I have no idea what you're talking about."

He feigned an innocent look that Eric found comical. "Not to be rude, but I need food. Aaron gave me a workout this morning and I'm famished."

A choking sound caught in Evie's throat. "Are you serious right now?"

"Serious about the workout?" he asked, deliberately misconstruing what she meant, judging by the mischievous twinkle in his eyes. "Of course I'm serious. Though I didn't mean like lifting weights kind of workout . . . though I'm sure sex could be considered a form of cardio . . ."

"*Stop*," Evie said, doing her best to cut off her brother's ramblings.

Garrett merely laughed. "Oh, come on, Evie. Are you going to tell me that Mom didn't leave a basket of stuff in your cabin for the two of you to have fun with?"

Evie flushed beet red, and Eric answered for her.

"Yes, Lauren did. It was very thoughtful of her." Especially since he and Evie had already enjoyed a few things from the basket.

Garrett smirked at Eric. "It's one of the perks of having hip, modern-thinking parents who encourage the idea that sex is natural and healthy and should be as pleasurable as possible."

Evie smacked her hand against her forehead. "*Please*, stop. I've already had my quota of embarrassment today and I can't take much more. Weren't you on your way to the buffet?"

Just as she asked the question, another man entered the room, glanced around, and headed toward the three of them. Judging by the way he was dressed in a pair of pale purple shorts and a matching tie-dyed tank top—not to mention the blatant way he was eyeing Eric—he assumed the guy belonged to Garrett.

"Evie, it's so good to see you." The other man kissed her on the cheek before turning to Eric and ogling him. "And who is this fine piece of . . . man candy?"

"Right?" Garrett nodded in agreement. "This is Evie's hot, gorgeous boyfriend, Eric."

"*Nice.*" Giving Eric a suave smile, Aaron extended his hand in greeting. "I'm Aaron, Garrett's better half."

Eric shook his hand, which was just as robust as Garrett's. "Nice to meet you."

"Likewise." Aaron released Eric's hand, a humor-filled smile curving his lips. "Just in case Lauren forgets to mention, all men signed up for the canoe race have to go shirtless."

Garrett nodded solemnly. "Yep. Truth."

Evie stared at the duo incredulously. "It's a lie," she assured Eric.

Aaron pretended to pout. "Why do you have to be such a killjoy, Evie?"

Garrett stepped closer, wrapped his hand around Eric's bicep, and gave it a squeeze. Eric was so startled by the action that he had no idea what to say to Evie's brother because he had no clue why he'd touched him.

She, however, had no problem coming up with words. "*What* are you doing?"

Garrett shrugged unrepentantly. "Just testing to see what Aaron and I are up against at the canoe race. Your man has some impressive muscles. Just sayin'," he said, following that up with a wink.

Eric shook his head and laughed. "Thank you?"

"Oh, you're most welcome." Garrett looped his arm through Aaron's. "And now, we need food before I waste away to nothing. See you two out on the lake for the race."

With a finger wave in their direction, the two of them headed toward the buffet, and beside him, Evie released a long, defeated groan. "God, I am *so* sorry. My family is insane."

"Stop apologizing," he said, tucking a wayward strand of hair behind her ear, even if it was just an excuse to touch her. "I love your family." He meant it. He loved that they were close and open with each other, happy, and not afraid to show how much they cared for one another.

She looked up at him with compassionate eyes. "I'm sorry if this is hard for you."

He knew she probably meant the sibling relationship, but surprisingly it wasn't difficult to watch their banter and close bond. "It's not hard at all," he assured her, then leaned closer. "And if you apologize for something one more time, I'm going to use those handcuffs on you when we get back to the cabin and give you a spanking."

Desire warmed in her eyes, telling him without words that she wasn't opposed to the idea. She cleared her throat. "I . . . uh, think we should go eat. *Food,*" she clarified before he could make a dirty remark, which had been on the tip of his tongue. "We should go eat food . . . breakfast stuff."

He chuckled, because he found her so damn

irresistible. "Yes, we should."

Grabbing her hand, he led the way to the buffet, grateful when there were no more interruptions. He piled his plate high with scrambled eggs, bacon, and hash browns, and she opted for a bagel with cream cheese and fruit. They found an empty table away from where everyone was talking and set their plates down, then they each went for a cup of coffee and ate their meal without interruption.

Just as they finished and put their plates, utensils, and mugs in the bin that had been set out for dirty dishes, Lauren announced that breakfast would be cleared away in fifteen minutes, and the canoe race would start in an hour. The woman had an itinerary and she was sticking to it, Eric thought in amusement.

"Want to go hang out at the lake until the race starts?" he asked, taking her hand and walking toward the door, where other members of her family were starting to filter out, as well.

Smiling at him, she nodded. "Yeah, I'd like that."

She glanced ahead, and a few steps later, before they reached the exit, a young blonde woman walked in, with a guy following a few steps behind . . . like a well-trained dog, Eric thought.

"Shit," Evie muttered beneath her breath, her steps slowing in an attempt *not* to become the focal point of the couple who'd just entered. "And here I thought I was getting lucky and wouldn't have to deal with her until later."

Her, he already knew, was Raquel. Even if Evie hadn't said something, he would have pegged the privileged, snooty-looking blonde as her cousin. Physically, she was stunningly beautiful, no doubt about it. She wore a white, sheer cover-up that deliberately contrasted against the tiny black bikini she had on underneath, which barely covered the essentials. Eric wondered why she'd even bothered to wear it . . .unless she wanted eyes on her.

A few people greeted the two of them, and Raquel basically waited for everyone to come to her, like she was holding court. And Graham . . . well, he seemed to go along with whatever Raquel did or ordered him to do . . . like get her a plate of fruit because she was *starving*. The only thing that was missing was a finger snap, but the other man jumped to do her bidding, even though he didn't look happy about it.

"Interesting dynamic between the two of

them," he observed to Evie.

"Yeah, they couldn't be more opposite, but when you have a face and body like that, I suppose Graham could overlook a lot of other things."

Eric arched a debating brow. "Being a beautiful bitch doesn't make her any less of one. She's still a bitch."

Evie's mouth twitched with humor and appreciation. "Yes, I suppose that's true."

He gave her hand a reassuring squeeze. "Want to make a beeline for the door and deal with them later?"

"No." She exhaled a deep breath and shook her head. "No sense stretching out the inevitable. Let's get this over with so I can keep my distance from them the rest of the weekend." She looked at Eric, her chin lifting a few determined notches. "Besides, I've got this."

His heart knocked around in his chest a little bit at how fucking sexy her confidence was. "Damn straight you do." He couldn't wait to see how this played out. His money was on Evie coming out on top.

CHAPTER THIRTEEN

THE MOMENT RAQUEL noticed her and Eric, Evie braced herself for her first face-to-face with her cousin in three years. While Graham did Raquel's bidding at the fruit table, she sauntered their way, hips swaying seductively, her gaze all over Eric—probably wondering how Evie had landed such a gorgeous catch. A few feet away, Raquel finally looked at Evie, her eyes facetiously wide.

"Oh my God, Evelyn," she exclaimed, using the full name Evie hated while pressing a hand to the boob job she'd clearly had done in the past few years. "Just look at you!"

Her cousin left that passive-aggressive comment hanging, because it could have gone a few different ways ... that Evie looked good (mmm, probably not what she'd been going for), or she looked fat (that wouldn't have been the first time she'd said as much), or she just looked plain and boring. Evie was pretty certain that Raquel hadn't meant it in a flattering way, but to their family standing around, she really hadn't said anything derogatory, either.

Eric slid his arm around Evie's waist and pulled her close to his side. "She looks pretty fantastic, wouldn't you say?" he replied.

Raquel blinked at him, startled by the direct question that forced her to answer. "I, uh, yes, of course."

"I'm Eric Miller, Evie's boyfriend," he said, not bothering with the pleasantries of extending his hand. "And you are?"

Raquel gave him one of those sultry smiles that never failed to turn men to idiots in her presence. "I'm her cousin Raquel." Again, she looked at Evie, a feigned frown now marring her brows as if she couldn't exactly pinpoint what had changed . . . probably because nothing major had. "It's just been so long and you look . . . different."

There it was again. Different good or different bad?

Eric tightened the arm around Evie's waist. "You know, love will do that to a person . . . make them look happy and glowing and incredibly sexy." He said the last part on a low, unmistakably possessive growl while burying his face in Evie's neck.

Evie shivered as he placed a warm kiss on her skin, enjoying the moment and not caring that he was pouring it on thick, not when her cousin looked so bewildered and confused by his attention on Evie and not her.

Graham joined them, holding the small plate of various fruits Raquel had sent him for. His gaze met Evie's, and she was surprised to see a glimmer of regret in his eyes before he blinked and it was gone. "Hi, Evie. It's good to see you."

He sounded like he meant it, but she couldn't say the same. "Hi, Graham. This is my boyfriend, Eric Miller."

The two shook hands civilly, but Evie didn't miss the way Graham sized up Eric, which was ridiculous since he had zero rights to her anymore.

"I'm sure your mother told you that we're engaged," Raquel announced gleefully, thrusting her left hand out in front of Evie's face for her to see the huge rock on her finger.

Evie waited for her stomach to twist with any kind of negative emotion, but there was nothing. She wasn't envious. She wasn't angry. And there were no regrets. She honestly didn't care about these two and it was a liberating feeling.

"She did tell me," Evie replied, casting her gaze from her cousin to Graham, who looked incredibly uncomfortable with the conversation. "Congratulations. To the both of you."

Graham shifted on his feet, as if he wanted to be anywhere but there at the moment. But his fiancée wasn't done trying to get under Evie's skin.

Raquel gave her a look that was just shy of being pitiful. "Evelyn—"

"It's *Evie*," she interrupted, her tone firm and insistent. Her cousin's use of Evie's full, old-fashioned name, which she'd been given after her grandmother, was nothing more than a tactic to subtly put her down, and she was tired of being bullied. "Not Evelyn. *Evie*." Nobody, not even her parents, called her Evelyn.

"Oh. Okay," Raquel said, as if she'd been the offended one. "You don't have to get upset about it. I've *always* called you Evelyn."

"I know." She gave her cousin an uncompromising smile. "But from this second forward, it's Evie."

A slow crawl of pink tinged Raquel's cheeks, and Evie couldn't remember ever seeing her cousin embarrassed before. Then again, it was the first time she'd ever put Raquel in her place . . . and damn, it felt good. As for Graham, instead of reeling in his fiancée, he was staring at the ground like he wanted it to crack open and swallow him whole.

Raquel sighed and quickly shifted gears. "I know this situation can't be easy for you."

Oh, her cousin definitely didn't want it to be easy, that was for sure. "Why would you say that?" Evie asked, sounding confused.

"Well . . . because of your past with Graham, and him now being engaged to me—"

"Raquel," Graham said, cutting her off with a warning in his voice, proving that maybe he did have a little bit of a backbone when it came to her.

Her cousin crossed her arms over her ample chest and gave Graham an irritable look. "Well, I just don't want this weekend to be awkward."

And knowing Raquel, she wanted Evie to feel as out of place as possible. But Evie was done letting her cousin get under her skin or manipulate her emotions. That was in the past, and she wasn't going to let anyone make her feel insecure or uncertain about herself ever again.

"It's not awkward," Evie said, her voice strong and poised. "As you can see, I've moved on. We're all adults, Raquel. You two have your life, and I have mine, and actually, it's pretty damn great. I'm sure you two will have a wonderful life together."

Evie didn't miss the troubled look on Graham's face, but whatever the reason, it wasn't her concern.

"Oh," Raquel said, sounding almost . . . disappointed that she hadn't made Evie feel insignificant.

"We're heading down to the lake," Evie went on, putting an end to their conversation because she had nothing left to say to either of them. "We'll see you around."

On that note, Eric tucked her hand in his and led her out of the room. She caught sight of her grandpa sitting at a nearby table, drinking his cup of coffee, and he gave her a small, supportive nod that told her he was proud of her for standing up to her cousin.

"Here's the fruit you wanted," Evie heard Graham say to Raquel just as they reached the door.

Raquel made a loud sound of disgust. "Are you serious?" she said, her tone irritable. "Half the plate is melon, Graham. You know I *hate* melon."

She and Eric kept on walking, and as soon as they stepped outdoors, he turned to her, his face full of humor. "Jesus Christ, Evie. I hate to say this, but you dodged a major fucking bullet with that guy."

She laughed, feeling lighter than air.

Eric stopped walking and crouched down in front of her, hands on his knees, presenting her with his back. "Hop on. You deserve a ride down to the lake after that awesome smack-down."

Evie didn't hesitate like she normally would have, because Eric wouldn't have made the suggestion if he hadn't been capable of carrying her. So, she leapt onto his back, securing her arms over his shoulders to hold on, while he tucked his forearms beneath her thighs and anchored her legs tight around his waist.

"That's my girl," he praised, and started walking the short distance to the water, where the canoe race would be held soon.

Her heart squeezed tight in her chest. God, she wanted to be his girl. So badly. Being with Eric felt so good and right. Like nothing else ever had with any other guy. There was an easiness with him, and he made her feel confident and secure . . . and so damn desirable.

The moment was so relaxing, until her brother zoomed by her and Eric with Aaron piggybacked on his back.

"Race you two down to the lake!" Garrett yelled, already sounding out of breath. "Last one there is the rotten egg!"

Evie burst out laughing. "What is he, twelve?"

"Right now he is," Eric said, tightening his hold on her legs. "Hang on because *my* inner twelve-year-old has just accepted his challenge."

Evie let out a startled scream as Eric bolted across the grass. His stride was smooth, his body agile and strong, and they passed Garrett and Aaron in no time flat. When they reached the edge of the water, with Eric having won the race, Garrett collapsed to the ground, taking Aaron with him, while wheezing and trying to catch his breath.

"Jesus Christ, Evie," Garrett huffed out, his gaze staring at Eric in awe. "Your man is a goddamn beast!"

"Damn straight I am," Eric joked, and crouched down again so Evie could slide off his back. He wasn't even breathing hard, nor had he broken a sweat, like her brother had.

She and Eric sat down on the grass next to her brother and Aaron, since it would only be a little while before everyone gathered by the lake for the canoe race. Garrett, whose breathing had finally evened out, glanced at Evie with a concerned look.

"Hey, everything okay with you and Raquel?" he asked. He might be the younger of the two of them, but he'd always been protective of her. "I saw you guys talking and she looked like she was being a . . . well, not nice," he amended. "Do you need your little brother to go back up to the lodge and kick some ass?"

Evie laughed as she drew her legs up and wrapped her arms around them. "No. It's all good. *I'm* good. I promise." She really was.

Garrett smirked as he eyed Eric like he *did* play for the same team, and thank God Eric took it all in stride. "It doesn't hurt that you have a fuck-hot boyfriend, while Raquel is stuck with a wuss who seems to have lost his dick and balls in the past three years."

Sadly, it was an apt description. She'd never seen Graham so passive before but she supposed Raquel had beaten him down, too, without him even realizing it. But that was

Graham's problem, not hers.

For the rest of the weekend, she had a fuck-hot boyfriend to enjoy.

"WE'RE GOING TO win!"

Evie glanced over at Garrett and Aaron, who were only one canoe length behind her and Eric, both of their red, sweaty faces creased with determination as they rowed for all they were worth. Most everyone else in the family who'd started with them in the race had fallen way behind with no real chance of catching up, including Graham and Raquel, who was screeching at her fiancé to go faster because she hated to lose.

Evie looked over her shoulder at Eric, who was sitting behind her since he was heavier and more muscular, so therefore he could apply more steering force to the canoe than she could. "They so aren't going to win!" she yelled to him as she dug her paddle deeper into the water to increase their speed.

"Damn, you really are competitive!" Eric grinned at her. "Then again, so am I, so let's do this!" His shoulders flexed as he made a hard, downward stroke with his paddle, which gained them a few more feet on the boys.

"Pump harder!" Evie's brother shouted to Aaron. "Pump faster!"

"That's what *he* said," Aaron replied, and snickered at his dirty joke. "And it's paddle harder, paddle faster, you dumb ass!"

"Whatever, just do it!" Garrett panted for breath. "You're not going to let a *girl* beat us, are you?"

"You underestimate your sister," Eric called out from behind her, his voice filled with laughter. "She's a badass and competitive as fuck!"

Thank goodness they were in the middle of the lake, far from everyone else in the race and all the other family members who'd brought folding chairs down to the shore to watch the fun event. Nobody could hear their bantering, so offending anyone with their choice of language wasn't an issue.

"Doesn't hurt that she has a beast sitting behind her!" Garrett grumbled.

Evie shook her head and cast another glance back at her brother. "Will you two stop being such pansies?"

"Jesus Christ, look at his arms!" Garrett

went on. "They are *bulging*!"

"I bet that's not all that's bulging," Aaron joked around his huffing and puffing as they valiantly tried to keep up.

"If you two spent more time concentrating on rowing, rather than eye-fucking my hot boyfriend, you *might* have a chance at winning!"

"He's so fucking distracting. It's not fair!" Garrett accused good-naturedly. "You're in front of us and all I can see are his broad shoulders and his tight ass!"

"We should use it as an incentive to row faster," Aaron suggested, nearly wheezing now. "You know, like a dangling carrot."

"A dangling carrot? Seriously?" Garrett's winded voice was ludicrous. "I'd rather have other kinds of dangling incentives!"

Behind Evie, Eric chuckled at their innuendo. He was such a good sport about it all, and Evie appreciated him letting her brother and Aaron have fun, even if it was at his expense.

The buoy up ahead that indicated the finish line drew closer and closer, and suddenly the power of the canoe gliding over the surface of the water increased exponentially, which was all Eric's doing, because honestly, Evie was exhausted and her arms were beginning to feel like limp noodles. His strength and stamina were impressive . . . but then again, she already knew that.

With Garrett and Aaron still shouting behind them, Evie and Eric's canoe passed the buoy, declaring them the winner, and she was so excited that she jumped up to her feet and raised her paddle over her head in victory while shouting a triumphant *hurrah*.

The sudden move caused the vessel to rock hard from side to side, and Eric's eyes widened in an *oh shit* moment as he stood up with his feet braced apart to stabilize the wobbling canoe. Despite his efforts, she lost her balance anyway, and he reached out and grabbed the front of her life jacket as she toppled overboard, taking him right along with her as they plunged into the cool water.

Seconds later, they bobbed to the surface of the lake, both of them laughing with Evie sputtering on the water she'd managed to swallow.

"I think I might need mouth-to-mouth!" she teased him, coughing.

With a sinful grin, he hooked his fingers in the front snaps of her life jacket and drew her to him. "I'm happy to oblige."

The fact that they were both wearing flotation devices made it hard to get close and stay that way, but Evie wrapped her legs around his waist, anchoring herself to him, while he framed her face in his hands and brought her lips to his for the hottest, sexiest form of CPR imaginable.

A few feet away from them, her brother and Aaron's canoe finally passed the buoy.

"Get a room, you two!" Garrett said, sounding completely beat.

Evie ignored him. For winning the race, they got bragging rights for the weekend, but right now, this decadent kiss was *her* prize, and she intended to savor every second of it.

AT TEN P.M. that Saturday night, Eric and Evie headed back to their cabin after spending a few hours with her family around the big bonfire located on the campgrounds for larger groups to enjoy. They sat around and her relatives brought up stories from other reunions, and as the older generation gradually retired for the evening, Garrett and Aaron took over with ridiculous horror stories, each one gorier than the last.

It had been a very long day, but Eric had a perma-smile on his face because he'd had a great time and so much fun . . . starting with winning the canoe race. Graham and Raquel had come in second to last, and she'd done nothing to disguise the fact that she was pissed that Graham hadn't tried harder. She'd stood up in her canoe wearing her skimpy bikini and no cover-up, most likely to berate Graham from a superior position, but as she'd waved her hands in the air dramatically while she screeched like a banshee, she'd ended up falling overboard instead.

Unlike Eric, who'd tried to catch Evie before she'd plunged into the lake, Graham just watched it happen, and when Raquel bobbed to the surface, he'd merely reached out his paddle to draw her back to the canoe, while she wailed that her hair was completely wet with gross water and her false lashes were ruined—hello, they were on a lake, for crying out loud—then demanded he take her back to shore, *right now*. Without a word, Graham had done as he was told.

A few of them had remained out on the lake, floating next to their canoes, enjoying the warm day and swimming and playing in the cool water. It was the kind of vacation Eric remembered spending with his parents and Trish during the summers ... when they'd been a family of four. He'd been hit with a wave of melancholy, but as he'd glanced over at Evie as she'd laughed at something her goofy brother had said, he was also struck with the realization of how relaxed he felt, how comfortable he was with her family, and how he wished that his time with Evie didn't have to end. But he was not that guy who could give her any kind of happily ever after, and she knew that about him.

After the canoe race, most of her other relatives did their own thing for the rest of the afternoon, while he and Evie spent time with her immediate family. They'd played cornhole and spent almost two hours talking to her grandpa, who was a fascinating, interesting man. They'd gone on a nature hike with Evie's father as a guide, with Garrett and Aaron adding hilarious side commentary. After dinner, they'd made and ate s'mores at the campfire—a first for him, but he'd definitely enjoyed licking the sticky marshmallow from Evie's fingers.

In truth, it was one of the best days of Eric's life since Trisha's death. The day had been filled with so much smiling and laughing and sense of family, and never once had he felt out of place.

As they entered their cabin, Evie turned on the light on the nightstand next to the bed and released a tired groan. "God, I'm absolutely exhausted."

Now that they were inside where there was light, he saw how pink her skin was on her face from their day in the sun, and as she pulled off her top, he could see that her shoulders and arms and anywhere else the one-piece bathing suit she was wearing had left her exposed were also a warm rose color. They'd put on sunscreen, but clearly they hadn't applied enough.

"And you're sunburnt," he told her.

Her eyes rounded in surprise. "Am I really?"

"A little bit, yes." He lightly skimmed his finger over the bridge of her nose and the tiny, almost miniscule brown dots that the sun had brought out. "And you have freckles."

"Ugh." She scrunched up her nose in disgust. "I hate when my freckles come out."

He grinned and brushed his thumb along her cheek, his pulse skipping a beat at the sweet way she looked up at him. "I like them. They're adorable." And Jesus, when did he start waxing poetic about a woman's complexion? "How about I rub some lotion on your shoulders and back where you're pink?"

She raised a suspicious brow. "I didn't see lotion in that basket, just flavored lubricant."

"Well, if I use the flavored lubricant, I can lick you afterwards. Anywhere you'd like." He waggled his brows for effect.

"You tempt me," she said with a cute sparkle in her eyes. "Actually, I have some real lotion in the bathroom, and now that you mention it, my skin does feel really warm. Maybe it'll help cool me down for the night."

"Consider me your personal masseuse tonight. Get undressed and get ready for these hands and fingers to make you moan in pleasure."

She giggled. "That sounds so dirty."

"Get your mind out of the gutter, Ms. Bennett," he said with a grin as he reached for the front of her shorts and unfastened the top button, then lowered the zipper, letting them drop to the floor. "It's a massage, nothing more ... unless you beg. Begging will get you just about anything you want, as you already know."

A sultry smile touched her lips. "Mmm. Yes, I do know that very well."

"Take off your bathing suit and make yourself comfortable on your stomach on the bed with the sheet up to your waist," he ordered gently. "I'll be right back with the lotion."

He left her alone for a few minutes, because he already knew if he watched her strip naked or saw her perfect bare ass, a massage would be secondary to fucking Evie because he wouldn't be able to resist her. At least with her half-covered, he'd hopefully have a fighting chance of not getting too distracted.

When he returned with the bottle of vanilla-scented lotion, she was in the position he'd requested, the covers in place, and her arms raised so that she could tuck her hands beneath her cheek. His eyes traced the slope of her back to the base of her spine, then over the lush curve of her ass beneath the sheet, making him remember how he'd taken her from behind that morning, and just like that, his dick was hard for her.

He shucked off his own clothes until he was in his boxer briefs, and ignoring the stiffy in his underwear, he moved onto the bed and strad-dled her hips from behind, making sure to keep his erection from riding the crease of her ass. He poured lotion into his hands, rubbing it between his palms to warm it before leaning over her and smoothing it across her slightly sunburned shoulders and along her arms.

He massaged her neck and across the taut tendons down the center of her back, then up again. Jesus, just touching her platonically turned him on. Or maybe it was the low, sexy, breathy groans she made as his fingers kneaded her muscles that made his stomach twist with desire and need. He reminded himself that this was about her, not him.

"You're spoiling me," she said on a soft, relaxed sigh. "This is the best boyfriend experience ever. I might have to hire you again just for your incredible masseuse skills."

He heard the teasing note in her increasingly lethargic voice as he continued to rub and soothe her upper body. She still thought he'd deliberately signed himself up for the Boyfriend Experience app as a side job, and he seriously thought about telling her the truth right then, because he wanted and needed to set things straight with her, but he didn't for two reasons. One, he didn't want to kill the mood for a serious conversation that required an explanation that would be more than one sentence, and two . . . her soft, barely perceptible snores told him that she was already out cold.

He smiled to himself, and after a few more light touches, he moved off of her to his side of the bed. And then he did something incredibly stupid . . . he watched her sleep. He stared at her beautiful, serene face. He thought about how perfectly she fit into his life and how happy and content he was when he was with her.

He felt a discernible shift inside of him, something he'd never experienced before with a woman, but it was quickly obliterated by fear. Whatever was happening inside him when it came to Evie, it scared the ever-loving shit out of him. So many emotions, so many feelings he couldn't and didn't want to handle or confront. So he did what he'd spent the past thirteen years perfecting . . . he pushed them deep down inside that dark place where they belonged. He couldn't give Evie everything she needed and deserved, so why even try?

He glanced away from her and reached for the cell phone on the nightstand that he'd left charging all day because he hadn't wanted to risk getting it wet or losing it. He'd never disconnected like that, and he honestly hadn't missed being attached to emails, texts, or social media.

Punching in his passcode, he saw that he had a text from Leo.

Just checking in. Everything is good here. Hope you're having a great time. Leo followed that up with a smirky smiley face. *Don't forget we have that two p.m. meeting Monday afternoon, so I'll see you in the office when you get back into town.*

Tomorrow, Sunday, was the Fourth of July, but Monday was a workday for Eric. He'd already talked to Evie on the drive up about leaving around eight in the morning on Monday so they'd get back to San Diego by noon and in plenty of time for his meeting.

He set the phone back down and released a deep breath. He had one more day with Evie. And he was selfish enough to take what he could from it, and her, even knowing he was going to walk away in the end.

CHAPTER FOURTEEN

T ANTRIC YOGA ... Yeah, Eric hadn't been thrilled about attending the spiritual, get-in-touch-with-your-emotions-and-sexuality session, but he'd promised Evie's mom that they'd be there. Something she'd been very excited about, and even though Evie assured him that they really didn't have to go, he hadn't wanted to disappoint Lauren. When the hell had he grown such a huge conscience?

It was a half hour. He could survive this.

There were eight couples sitting on mats on the floor in a room at the lodge, facing their partners, holding hands, their crossed knees intimately touching. There was Lauren and Gene, him and Evie, Garrett and Aaron, Graham and Raquel, and four other married relatives who'd been curious to learn all about the benefits of tantric yoga.

Calming, lyrical music played in the background while Lauren guided them all through breathing exercises in a soft, soothing voice as she talked about cherishing your body and your mind and harnessing your sexual energy to make orgasms more intense. Yeah . . . not really what Eric was into, but he followed along . . . including the part where they were supposed to stare into their partner's eyes.

Before long, he heard Raquel muttering beneath her breath about how stupid it all was and how bored she was . . . and while Eric would rather have been anywhere else, he wanted to tell Raquel to shut the fuck up and stop being so disrespectful to the couples trying to benefit from Lauren's lesson. It was just common courtesy.

Because there was no talking allowed, Evie rolled her eyes at her cousin's whiny complaints, and Eric winked at her as he caressed his thumb across the back of her hand. She smiled at him sweetly, shyly, and he wanted to lean forward and kiss her . . . which wasn't part of the exercise. Actually, holding back on your desires was the theme of Lauren's lesson, which she promised would create a spiritual bond that, when finally released through sexual intercourse, would heighten the physical and emotional connection between a couple.

"Keep staring deeply into your partner's eyes," Lauren instructed. "Feel their passion and desire. Let them feel yours. Open yourself completely, be vulnerable, and trust that they will do the same."

Eric kept his gaze on Evie's, following through on what was expected . . . but somewhere along the way, his sole focus became the woman sitting in front of him, as if the two of them were the only ones in the room. And suddenly, everything went from I'm-just-going-through-the-motions-until-this-session-is-over to something so intense he felt like he'd just been pushed over a cliff without a fucking parachute, because staring into Evie's vulnerable blue eyes was like staring into her soul. And what he saw there, what he felt deep inside himself shook him to his core.

She was a woman he could spend the rest of his life with. And he was never going to know what that was like.

"THE BEST WAY to skip a rock over the surface of the water is to first find a smooth stone like this one that's about the size of your palm."

Evie held up the flat stone she'd found at the lake's shore, where she and Eric had wandered down to after lunch.

"Like this one?" he asked, scooping up a similar-looking rock and showing it to her before giving her a sinful smile that made her belly flutter. "Except my palm is *much* bigger than yours."

"I'm well aware of that," she murmured, unable to forget how those big hands had covered her breasts, how his long fingers had done wicked things to her body. "But this is about finding a well-balanced stone . . . and not about your sexual prowess."

He chuckled and arched a brow. "I might have sex on the brain after that Tantric exercise. Though I'm not a fan of the whole holding back on my desires when I could easily spend the afternoon doing really hot, dirty things to you."

She laughed, because she knew he was trying to make light of the earlier session. They'd been following her mother's instructions to breathe and relax, to look into each other's eyes, to let their partner feel their passion, longing, and need and be open and vulnerable to each other.

She hadn't expected Eric to take any of it seriously, but there had been a definite change in him as he'd stared into her eyes and they'd connected on a deeper level than just superficial attraction. For a few intriguing minutes, it was as though he'd allowed himself to drop those emotional defenses he'd built around himself when his sister had died, and then panicked when it all became too much to deal with.

Because he clearly had years of practice, he'd refortified those protective walls and opted to joke about it now. But the whole encounter had left Evie's heart feeling more for this man than she ever could have imagined a week ago when she'd clicked on his profile app. She wasn't an insta-love kind of girl, but there was no denying that she was falling hard and fast for Eric . . . which had heartbreak written all over it.

She went back to instructing him how to skim a stone the way her grandfather had taught her and Garrett when they were younger. She'd been ten years old and it hadn't taken her long to learn the right grip, angle, and release to throw the rock, and as she did so now, it bounced nine times across the surface of the lake before finally sinking.

"That's impressive and I suck at this," he

said as his own rock made a sad plopping sound into the water as he tried to follow her advice.

She found it amusing that the hot, athletic guy who was the total package didn't have the coordination to skim a stone. "The flat part of the rock needs to hit the water parallel to the surface. It just takes practice."

He bent down to retrieve another rock and positioned his fingers the way she'd told him to. "I remember being on vacation with my parents and Trisha before she got sick, and my dad tried teaching us to skim stones. He was patient, but I just couldn't get the hang of it back then, either." He laughed.

While Eric had told Evie about his sister's illness and death, he'd pretty much glossed over his parents, except for the fact that they'd shut down emotionally after Trisha's passing and eventually divorced. "Where are your parents now?" she asked.

Surprisingly, he didn't hesitate to share. "Well, after they divorced, my dad ended up meeting someone else. He's remarried and is now living in Arizona. I talk to him occasionally and visit when I can. And the best way I can describe my mom is that she's spent the past thirteen years isolating herself and mourning my sister's death. She still lives in the same house my sister and I grew up in. She works in a nursery taking care of the plants and flowers, and I make it a point of having dinner with her every Sunday when I can."

Evie felt bad that his mom was spending *this* Sunday alone since Eric was here with her. She remembered him mentioning his mother falling into a deep depression and him feeling shut out. "Is she still battling with depression?"

"Honestly, it's not as bad as it was. She's on meds and functioning, and she has good days and bad days, but I know she's lonely." He lowered his head, his gaze on the way he was absently flipping the stone between his fingers. "It's really sad, but my mom lost a lot of her close friends because she wouldn't take their calls or see them when they stopped by. She essentially pushed them out of her life when Trisha died."

He glanced at Evie, his eyes a little optimistic. "However, I think she's going to try to reconnect with a friend she saw recently at work who asked her to lunch. God, I really do hope she's going to try and make the effort, because when she told me about it, I saw a spark of my old mom again, and she needs more in her life than her garden and my sister's memory."

"After thirteen years, that has to be really hard," she said, as a warm afternoon breeze filtered through her hair. "Opening yourself up again to friendships that have fallen by the wayside can't be easy."

"I completely agree. She's nervous, rightly so, because so much has changed." He shook his head wistfully. "She used to be this vibrant, outgoing woman who kept up her appearance, and now she's someone who no longer cares about her looks. My mom is in her fifties, but she let her hair go, and with all the gray, she looks like she's closer to sixty. I get the feeling that bothers her and is part of the reason she's hesitant to put herself back out there again."

An idea came to mind, one that excited Evie. "Eric, why don't you bring your mother into the salon?" she suggested. "I'll give her a haircut and color the gray and help give her some confidence back. Kind of what I do for the women on Beautiful You day."

He blinked at her in surprise at the suggestion, then a slow, grateful smile lifted his lips. "That's a fantastic idea."

"Then consider it done." She was happy to give his mother a small makeover, just a little something to make her feel beautiful and good about herself again. "When I get back to work, I'll look at my schedule and give you a time when I have an opening this next week."

"Okay," he agreed, though neither of them brought up the fact that this temporary, fake relationship between them would be done and over with by then. Her offer was strictly about building his mother's self-esteem back up, because that's what she enjoyed doing, and nothing more.

Out of the corner of her eye, Evie saw a monarch butterfly and focused on that instead. "Look at that. I hardly see butterflies anymore," she mused, smiling as it fluttered their way.

Beside her, Eric stilled, his expression amazed. "My sister," he said, his voice low.

She had no idea what he was talking about. "Your sister?" she asked in confusion.

His gaze never left the butterfly, which seemed to dance playfully in the air a few feet away from them. "Growing up, Trisha was obsessed with butterflies. She loved them, and they always seemed to gravitate to her. They hated me, probably because I was a stupid kid who tried swatting them away. And now . . . whenever I see them, I know it's Trisha's way of letting me know she's around and watching over me."

Oh, wow. His explanation made Evie's heart swell in her chest. The wonder and awe with which he watched the butterfly caused her throat to tighten with emotion. And when he slowly moved up behind Evie, pressing his body intimately close, then lifted her hand straight out with his palm cupping hers, she felt like he was sharing a piece of his heart with her.

"Hey, Trish," he cajoled softly while sliding an arm around Evie's waist to bring their bodies flush, making them one instead of two. "Come and meet Evie."

The butterfly dipped and teased and swirled around the two of them before finally settling in the palm of Evie's hand, its beautiful wings coming to rest together. She gasped in shock and sheer wonder at the sight. Butterflies did not randomly land on people . . . yet this one trusted her and Eric enough to rest gently in their joined hands.

With Eric's chest pressing against her back, she could feel him breathing, slow and calm, savoring the rare moment just as much as she was, and everything it meant to her. The moment was so poignant it choked her up.

After a short while, the butterfly gently flapped its wings and took off, and Eric buried his face against Evie's neck, his mouth near her ear. "She would have liked you," he whispered, the sadness in his voice tugging on her heart.

Evie swallowed hard to keep her own emotions at bay. She was certain she would have liked Trisha, too.

Eric gradually released Evie, and when she glanced at him, she found his expression unreadable, as if he'd realized how deeply emotional and intimate the moment had been and was trying to recover. Evie understood. She was feeling a bit off-balance, as well.

He exhaled a deep breath. "I'm going to head up to the lodge to get a bottled water. Would you like one?"

"Yeah, that sounds good." She considered joining him, but after everything he'd just shared, about his mother and then the butterfly, she figured he could use a little time alone with his thoughts. And truthfully, she didn't mind having a few minutes with hers.

"I'll be right back."

He walked up the pathway toward the lodge, and she continued skipping stones, which she found incredibly relaxing. It was early afternoon, and while there were people floating out on the lake and meandering around the resort area, it was quiet where she was, and she soaked it in before they were scheduled to meet up with the rest of the family for dinner and the Fourth of July fireworks later that evening.

Less than a few minutes passed before she heard footsteps behind her. Surprised that Eric was back so soon, she turned around and was even more startled to see Graham walking toward her . . . without Raquel anywhere around.

Unease crept through her. She had no desire to be alone with Graham. Not that she was afraid of him, she just didn't trust him . . . or like him much anymore.

Evie narrowed her gaze. "Where's Raquel?" she asked when he reached her, putting up that barrier between them—the fact that he had a fiancée and yet here he was alone with Evie.

"She's at our cabin. She had a migraine and wanted to take a nap." He pushed his hands into the front pockets of his khaki shorts. "I saw you standing out here by yourself and wanted to talk to you without either of our significant others around."

Evie crossed her arms over her chest. "I

don't think Raquel would like seeing you hanging out with me, and quite honestly, I don't think you and I have anything left to say to one another."

He exhaled a deep breath and met her gaze, the determination she saw swirling in the depths making her uncomfortable. "Evie . . . I just wanted to apologize about what happened in the past."

She arched a brow and didn't bother making anything easy on him. "You mean having an affair with my cousin while you were in a relationship with me?"

He clenched his jaw at her blatant, unvarnished response. "Clearly, that, yes," he admitted, his spine stiffening. "I have a lot of regrets about what I did and the choices I made. I'd do anything to go back and change what happened because it should be you I'm marrying, not Raquel. I'm so fucking miserable. If there is still any chance left between us . . ." He spoke quickly, then let the words trail off, but it was clear what he was asking.

He wanted her back, and Evie had to resist the urge to laugh in his face. "Miserable or not, you asked Raquel to marry you. You put a ring on her finger, which is a commitment, Graham." Clearly, something he had no concept of.

"Raquel pressured me for the engagement," he said defensively. "I'd leave her in a heartbeat if you and I could go back to what we had together."

She stared at Graham, wondering if he was for real. But he looked dead serious, and she was so done being used by men. After being treated like a queen by Eric this weekend, she knew she'd never settle for anything less in the future.

"Just in case it's slipped your mind, what we had together was three years that ended in lies, deceit, and betrayal, and that dishonesty negates anything good that came before," Evie said, watching as a spark of irritation flashed in his gaze, which had no right being there when she'd been the one wronged. "And the fact that you'd even think I'd want you back or take you back is ludicrous. I don't want you, and I have more pride and self-worth than that."

Her words were equivalent of the slap across his face that she'd never had the chance to give him when the truth had come out, and he knew it, too.

"Yeah . . . she really does have more pride and self-worth than that," Eric said casually from behind them as he strolled in their direction, clearly having heard their conversation. When he reached Evie, he handed her one of the bottles of water, then slipped his arm around her waist and pulled her close. "I mean, why would she settle for a hot dog when she has filet mignon on her plate to eat?"

Graham's face reddened at the insult, and Evie had to bite her bottom lip to keep a lid on the snicker threatening to spill out of her. Realizing that Graham was no match for Eric, verbally or physically, he spun around and strode off toward the cabins.

Once he was out of hearing range, Evie glanced at Eric in pure amusement. "Filet mignon? Seriously?"

"Damn straight I'm serious," he said, grinning at her. "I'm Grade A Prime beef all the way, baby. Every. Single. Inch."

She couldn't disagree, and laughed at his quip. God, she was going to miss his humor after this weekend. Who was she kidding? She was going to miss *everything* about him.

CHAPTER FIFTEEN

THE BRIGHT, COLORFUL fireworks bursting across the dark night summer sky signaled the end to the family reunion weekend. Evie sat on a blanket between Eric's updrawn knees, leaning back against his chest with his arms wrapped around her midsection. She felt both contentment and sadness . . . two highly conflicting emotions, and unfortunately, she knew which one was going to ultimately win. The contentment she felt in Eric's arms was temporary. The sadness would be far longer lasting once they parted ways tomorrow.

Never would she have ever believed that she'd fall for a guy who'd never had a girlfriend, avoided commitment like the plague, and had a profile on a Boyfriend Experience app. Those were three solid reasons why bringing Eric to the family reunion should have been simple, casual, and uncomplicated, for both of them. A one-and-done transaction with an easy goodbye when they returned home and to their separate lives.

But there was nothing simple or straight-forward about her feelings for Eric. He was funny and caring and affectionate. But he was also a complex man beneath that easygoing charm, with scars and fears that ran deep. And after he'd spent thirteen years living his life one way to make sure he didn't hurt either himself or any woman the way his sister's death had shattered him, changing that mindset would be like moving a mountain.

But God, she wanted to try so badly with him, but she was scared, too. Not of the possibility of him someday getting sick like his sister, but spending who knew how many years trying to find someone who affected her so deeply, so completely, as he did. A man who felt like he was meant just for her, because they were so in sync, so compatible, that they just belonged together and everything else would work itself out. But he wasn't willing to take that chance, nor would she ever force him to.

For her, there would be life before Eric . . . and life after him. And she already knew that the latter was going to be so much worse than the former.

The fireworks finally died down, and everyone stood up and collected their blankets and belongings. Another half an hour of hugs and goodbyes to family and relatives, and promises to Evie's parents that they'd visit soon—untrue since she planned to inform her mom and dad in a few weeks that the two of them had broken up—and she and Eric were heading back to their cabin. Once inside, they started packing their bags since they were getting an early morning start back to San Diego, both of them quiet as they gathered up their things.

Wanting to break the uncomfortable silence, Evie glanced over at Eric as he took his T-shirts from the dresser drawer and set them in his bag. "Once we get back home, I'll be sure to leave you a glowing review on the beta version of the Boyfriend Experience app," she said, even though the thought of him dating other women made her feel a little stabby, as well as made her heart die a bit inside. "You were an awesome fake boyfriend."

He stopped moving and looked at her, his expression suddenly serious. "Evie, I never put myself on the app to be hired out," he said, surprising her. "The owner, Dylan Stone, who is a friend of mine, did it as a joke and without my knowledge. And I'm not a chauffeur. I own a car service company with a friend."

What? She shook her head in confusion as she tried to process everything he'd just said. "I'm not sure I understand."

"I'm not actually a boyfriend for hire. I don't hire out my boyfriend services for money on a regular basis, or as a side job, and I sure as hell won't do it again once we get back home. You were my first, last, and only 'client.'"

She rubbed her forehead where a frown had formed. "I'm still not following."

He walked over to where she was standing on the other side of the bed, tucking a strand of hair behind her ear. "I suppose I owe you an apology, but I can't say I'm sorry about this weekend with you." He picked up her hands in his. "Dylan signed me up for the app behind my back, and when I realized what he'd done, I wasn't going to accept your request. But then he swiped my phone and answered your notification before I realized what he was doing and accepted your coffee date the next morning on my behalf."

"And still . . . you could have canceled."

"I was going to explain everything in person at the coffee shop, but then I met you and . . .

well, I couldn't say no. I didn't want to say no."
His sincerity rang true in his tone. "You fascinated me like no other woman ever has, and
honestly I was hooked. I thought it would be
fun and nothing serious . . . but I never counted
on you getting under my skin, Evie."

She swallowed hard at what he'd just admitted and confirmed about his feelings toward
her. She wasn't angry about him not telling her
the truth from the beginning, or even upset,
because he'd done nothing malicious. He didn't
sign up for the app . . . but he'd gone through
with the Boyfriend Experience once he'd met
her. Because she'd fascinated him and he'd been
hooked.

"It probably makes me a certified asshole
for—"

She covered his mouth with her hand. "It
doesn't make you anything of the sort. You've
been amazing and more than I ever could have
asked for in a fake boyfriend," she teased, then
realized she didn't want to go back to the city
with regrets, which meant putting her heart on
the line and letting the chips fall where they
might.

"You did your job exceptionally well, and
I'd do anything to make what's between us as

real as what I think we're both feeling."

He squeezed his eyes shut for a second, his expression pained. "Fuck . . ." he swore beneath his breath, and when he opened his eyes again, they were filled with anguish. "This wasn't supposed to happen. I wasn't supposed to fall for you."

"But we both fell. Together. And there's no reason why we can't try and make this work when we get back to San Diego," she said hopefully, knowing she was wearing her heart and emotions on her sleeve like she never had before.

He bit down on the inside of his cheek. She prayed with everything in her that he was considering what she said. But looking into his eyes, she knew the moment he shut down any possibility of a future together.

"I'd like to think we'd at least be friends after this," he said quietly.

God, that hurt. So much. "I can't make that promise, Eric." Actually, she *wouldn't* make that promise and decided to risk everything for a chance to be with him. "I feel too much for you and I can't be friends with someone I . . . love," she admitted, knowing it was true. "Knowing I'll never really have you. Ever."

He groaned, the sound low and tortured.

She knew what his issues were without him saying a word. Knew why he'd never allowed his emotions to get involved with any woman, and addressed those concerns. "Eric, I would gladly take another week with you, a month, a year . . . rather than nothing at all. I would take *anything* with you, even knowing what the risks are, because I wouldn't want to live our life, our future, thinking about what-ifs that may never happen."

A muscle in his jaw clenched tight. "I'm not going to do that to you, Evie."

"It's *my* choice to make," she argued.

He let go of her hands and pushed his fingers through her hair, forcing her head back, and pinned her with his stare. "No, it's *mine*," he countered, his tone brusque and irritable to cover the underlying pain she saw in his eyes.

Before she could say anything more, he crushed his mouth to hers, the taste of his kiss raw and emotional and demanding. It started angry and punishing, his hands suddenly tearing away her clothes to get her naked, and she helped him do the same, her body already wet and eager and hungry for the feel of him inside her.

He pushed her back on the bed, rolled on a

condom, then came over her, grabbing her hands and pinning them at the sides of her head. His cock found her core, and he lined himself up and drove so deep inside her in one hard thrust he impaled her completely. She arched beneath him and cried out as he claimed her, rough and desperate and without his normal finesse.

When she didn't fight back and instead wrapped her legs tight around his waist and just let him take whatever he needed from her, even if it was just this physical release to stave off the avalanche of emotions he was feeling, something seemed to switch inside him. His thrusts gradually slowed, gentled, as if he was now savoring what he'd never have again.

His fingers tightened around her wrists, and he buried his face in her neck, his breathing ragged as he dragged the length of his shaft back out, then entered her again in one long, pleasurable stroke that made her thighs quiver against his hips. She closed her eyes as his warm male scent wrapped around her, and she imprinted it in her memory to recall in the lonely nights ahead. With each slow downward grind against her sex, desire pulsed through her veins, thick and hot, pushing her closer to the orgasm building inside her.

"I'm sorry, Evie," he whispered jaggedly against her throat, sounding so broken inside it brought tears to her eyes. "I'm so fucking sorry."

She knew he wasn't apologizing for the barbaric way he'd just fucked her, but rather his inability to take that ultimate risk for her and with her. He coaxed them both toward orgasm—heat, softness, and slick friction adding to the pleasurable climb—and he lifted his head and watched her face as she came beneath him, then looked deeply into her eyes before his entire body shuddered with his own release.

And when he kissed her a few minutes later, it tasted like goodbye.

ERIC WALKED INTO the office an hour before the scheduled Monday afternoon meeting with Leo and a client. He'd just dropped Evie off at her place after a long, quiet car ride back to San Diego. They both knew there was nothing left to talk about since he'd pretty much shut down any possibility of a real relationship with Evie the night before—for her own good, he told himself, forcing himself to believe the words.

The thought of never seeing her again cut him like a knife, and the laceration felt fresh and raw. His greatest fear was that this particular wound would never heal, because as crazy as it was to even him, he loved her and always would. Yes, he loved her . . . There was no other explanation for the deep, emotional connection he'd felt with her. But none of that changed the fact that he was doing what was best for Evie, even if she didn't agree, and that took precedence over his own feelings toward her.

He was glad that Heather wasn't at her desk, because he wasn't in the mood to chat or give anyone a rundown of his weekend as a boyfriend for hire. He went to his office, booted up his computer, and reviewed the emails relating to the upcoming meeting so he'd be refreshed and prepared for their presentation.

A few minutes later, Leo walked into his office. "Hey, I thought I heard you come in," he said, taking a seat in one of the chairs in front of Eric's desk. "How did the weekend go?"

"I don't want to talk about it." Eric was not an overtly emotional guy to begin with, let alone one who talked about his feelings with another dude. And the fact that he was feeling things he'd never experienced before had him so fucking confused and disconcerted he wouldn't even know where to begin.

Leo winced sympathetically. "That bad, huh?"

Eric stared at his friend, giving him one of his leave-me-the-fuck-alone glares to get his point across. Leo knew about his sister's death, but he had no idea what Eric's fears were. In fact, the only person in the world he'd ever shared those doubts and concerns with up to this point was Evie. Not even his mother knew the research he'd done on fraternal twins and cancer, which had always kept him from letting any kind of relationship develop with a woman.

With Evie, though, he hadn't stood a chance. He'd never known such a sweet, kind, selfless woman like her . . . nor had he ever been inclined to share the kind of things that he had with Evie because it felt right. Because *she* felt right.

"Oh, shit." Leo smirked knowingly. "Did you actually *fall* for her?"

"What part of 'I don't want to talk about it' don't you fucking understand?" he asked through gritted teeth.

Amusement danced in his partner's eyes. "The part that tells me some woman actually managed to do what dozens before her never could."

"Which is?" Eric asked before he thought better of it.

"Broke through to your walled-off heart." Leo suddenly turned more serious. "However, you don't seem happy about it, which is more of a normal reaction to falling for someone, which concerns me."

"No need to be concerned," he assured his friend. "I'm fine."

He was far from fine. He was torn up inside and wondered when he'd feel normal again. If ever. Jesus.

"Okay." Leo stood to go, then hesitated, pushing his hands into the front pockets of his khakis. "One last thing and I'll leave it alone. I almost lost Peyton because I thought letting her go was what was best for her, and I was afraid to trust that what I was feeling would last after what happened with my ex. All I can say is thank God I pulled my head out of my ass in time to realize that Peyton is the best thing that has ever happened to me, and now, I can't imagine my life without her in it."

But this was different, Eric thought. What about Evie's life if something happened to him?

Yet he heard his friend loud and clear, and

as Leo turned and walked out of the office, he left Eric even more confused than ever.

The cellphone on his desk buzzed with a text message, and he glanced at the screen, seeing that it was from Evie. His heart skipped a hopeful beat in his chest at the sight of her name, then fell flat when he read her note.

I have an opening Thursday afternoon at two p.m. for your mom.

So polite and cordial, like they hadn't spent the weekend sharing their deepest, most intimate secrets. Like he hadn't been so deep inside her, where everything felt so damn perfect and right and unlike anything he'd ever experienced with any woman before.

He dragged his fingers through his hair, irritation quickly adding a layer to his already bad mood. What did he expect from Evie after rejecting her when she'd offered him her heart? She'd made it clear that they wouldn't be casual friends who stayed in contact after they went their separate ways, and he had to respect her request.

He'd made his choice, and now he had to live with the consequences.

Alone.

CHAPTER SIXTEEN

HOW WAS IT possible for Evie to both anticipate and dread seeing Eric when he dropped his mom off at the salon Thursday afternoon? The conflicting emotions had her stomach twisting and turning. Through the large windows in front of the shop, she saw him walking with a woman she assumed was his mother, Ginny, lightly holding her elbow in a gesture Evie found incredibly sweet because it was clear how much he cared about his mom.

Ginny Miller definitely looked a little nervous and uncertain about her visit to Evie's salon. From what Eric had told her, it had been years since she'd done anything with her hair, and while Evie knew that his mother was aware of the appointment her son had made for her, she was also certain that Ginny had no idea what to expect, which was why she appeared so anxious.

The other woman had nothing to worry

about, because Evie had already selected a few possible hairstyles and hair colors for the two of them to discuss. Nothing radical or too extreme. She wanted Ginny to be happy with whatever new look she ended up with.

As soon as Eric stepped into the reception area, Evie felt as though his presence had sucked all the air from her lungs. Her heart squeezed painfully tight at seeing the man who fulfilled everything on her checklist but would never be a part of her life in the way she'd hoped. She pasted on an amicable smile and headed in their direction, trying to remain professional when all she wanted to do was throw herself in his arms because that's how much she'd missed him.

"Hi, Eric," she said, hating the slight quiver she heard in her own voice, along with the fact that she was probably wearing her broken heart on her sleeve.

"Evie." He nodded in greeting, and even though she could see how guarded and reserved he was, his eyes told a different story.

They looked at her with the same kind of misery she'd been dealing with the past four days, and she had to force her attention away from him and to the woman at his side before the tears she'd managed to keep tucked away during working hours threatened to burst free. No, she only allowed herself to indulge in those crying jags at night.

"You must be Eric's mom, Ginny," Evie said, reaching out to gently shake the woman's hand. "It's so nice to meet you and I'm excited to see what we can do to make you feel like a million bucks by the time you leave today."

Ginny laughed lightly and self-consciously touched the wavy ends of her hair. "At this point, feeling like a hundred bucks would be amazing."

The other woman had her son's wry sense of humor and his kind eyes. "We only work in the millions here, so get ready to have your socks knocked off." She shifted her gaze back to Eric, fighting to remain composed and businesslike. "Give me about three hours with her."

"Perfect." He smiled, but the sentiment didn't erase the pain in his eyes. "I'll be back to pick her up around five."

As soon as he left the salon, Evie felt as though she could breathe and think again. She led his mom over to her station, and once she had Ginny settled in her chair, she brought out the magazines she'd ear-marked with a few styles for Ginny to choose from. She selected a pretty layered bob that Evie assured her would look great with the shape of her face and her jawline, and together they narrowed down the color to a warm chestnut shade that would cover the gray and give her a hint of red high-lights.

Then Evie got to work, first painting sections of Ginny's hair with the dye, aware of the fact that the other woman was looking at her more curiously now in the mirror.

"So you're the girl that Eric went to Santa Barbara with last weekend."

It wasn't a question, but a statement, which meant Eric had mentioned her to his mother as more than a hairdresser who was going to do her hair. Honestly, Evie was surprised that he'd told his mom as much, but not knowing if Ginny knew the whole story about how Evie had met her son through the Boyfriend Experience app, she decided to just let Ginny lead the conversation and reveal what *she* knew.

"Yes, I am," she replied, giving nothing away as she sectioned off another part of Ginny's hair.

"I thought maybe the two of you were dating."

"No." Evie glanced in the mirror to meet the other woman's gaze and forced a smile. "We're just friends."

"You know, he told me the same thing, but I just saw with my own eyes the way he was looking at you . . . and the way you were looking at him, and I know I'm really rusty and out of the game when it comes to having strong feelings for someone, but from my perspective, and it's probably none of my business, but it seems like there is more between the two of you than just friendship."

Evie swallowed hard, knowing she had to be careful with her reply yet be true to herself, as well. "I care for your son. A lot. And I suppose it could be something more than friendship, except he's a little gun-shy when it comes to a long-term relationship." And that was putting it mildly. Evie didn't stand a chance against all the reasons Eric believed they couldn't be together.

Ginny cast her gaze downward, her expression dismayed, as if she blamed herself for his inability to commit. "He's always been that way. If he's ever had a girlfriend, I've never met one. And it makes me sad."

It made Evie incredibly sad, too. But what

could she say to that? Evie continued the coloring process. Dipping the brush into the dye. Applying it to her hair. Another section, repeat process.

Ginny raised her eyes back to their reflection in the mirror, meeting and searching Evie's eyes as though she'd found someone who might understand the family situation and, maybe, her son.

"Did he tell you about Trisha?" she finally asked, a flicker of grief passing across her features.

Evie tried not to appear startled, because she never would have anticipated Ginny bringing up something so personal. Then again, maybe she'd kept everything bottled up for so long and now saw something in Evie—like a connection to her son that she, herself, didn't have—that made her want to open up about the past. "Yes, he did."

"We all took her death differently, and I'm beginning to realize that I've spent way too many years hanging on to the past and not being present in Eric's life like I should have been." Her voice cracked slightly, her anguish nearly palpable. "I know I've missed out on so much by letting my grief over Trisha's death consume me, and my biggest fear is that he won't be able to forgive me for shutting him out when he needed me the most. How does a mom fix something like that?"

She sounded so ashamed, and Evie's heart went out to Ginny. She'd made mistakes but she clearly loved her son. And she wanted to make amends. Evie gave her the only guidance she could without being too intrusive. "You start by being present in his life. By talking to him about things you're feeling, even if the topics are difficult ones to address. Eric just needs to know you're there for him."

"You sound like my therapist," Ginny said, clearly trying to make light of the situation.

Evie smiled at the other woman. "Then maybe you should take their advice and apply it to your relationship with Eric. He's one of the best men I've ever known, and he's going to love you and forgive you and be there for you no matter what's happened between the two of you, or in the past."

"You know that about him?" she asked quietly, hopefully.

"I do," she assured Ginny as she finished with the hair dye. Eric's heart might have been shattered, but his kind, compassionate soul spoke for itself. She'd seen so many facets of his personality last weekend to know exactly what kind of sincere, honorable, humble man he was, even if he didn't believe it himself.

"All I want is him to be happy," Ginny said candidly. "To meet a girl and fall in love like he deserves. I hoped since he'd mentioned you that maybe that had finally happened."

A swell of emotion tightened in Evie's throat, and all she could manage was a shake of her head to indicate a reply of no. It wasn't her place to explain Eric's reasons for not wanting to commit to Evie, to his mother.

When she finally felt as though she could talk again, she said, "I'm going to have you sit here in my chair for about a half hour to let the color develop." She reached for a nearby magazine and handed it to Ginny to read if she wanted. "I'm going to go gather some other things I need and be back in a few minutes."

She walked to Scarlett's station, grateful that her friend was in a room giving a client a facial so she didn't see everything written all over Evie's face and hound her to talk. She'd been avoiding conversation with both Scarlett and Jessica about Eric, and she knew her time was limited. She grabbed a few makeup items to use on Ginny after her hair was done, and when Evie returned to her station, their conversation turned to other things. Like Ginny's job at a nursery and how much she loved nurturing plants and flowers. She even told Evie about meeting the friend from long ago for lunch.

By the time the appointment was finished and Evie turned Ginny around to look at herself in the mirror to see the full effect of everything Evie had done—from the rich color of her hair, the soft, layered bob, to the light application of makeup on her face—the other woman gasped audibly and tears filled her eyes.

"Oh my God," Ginny whispered in wonder and awe as she stared at her reflection. "I look . . ."

It was as if she couldn't bring herself to say the words, so Evie smiled and supplied them for her. "Absolutely beautiful."

A tremulous smile touched Ginny's lips, and her eyes shone with undeniable joy. "Yes, I do look beautiful. And about ten years younger, too. I never should have let myself go for so long."

"Don't focus on the past and things you can't change, Ginny," Evie said, hoping someday she'd be able to take her own advice and apply it to her and Eric, once her heart had time to mend. "Just keep looking toward the future and all the good things waiting to happen."

Ginny grabbed her hand, squeezing it tight, her gaze filled with gratitude. "Thank you, Evie. For everything."

Evie knew what she meant . . . the makeover and for letting her talk about her family and even the advice Evie had issued. "You're welcome."

If Evie was able to do anything for Eric, helping his mother repair her relationship with her son would be her gift to him.

ERIC COULDN'T STOP looking over at the woman sitting in the passenger seat of his car, still trying to process how Evie had taken his mother's plain, dowdy appearance and had turned her into a stunning, radiant, more confident person in the span of three hours.

When he'd walked into the salon at five p.m. to pick up his mom, he'd done a double take when his gaze had skimmed by her sitting in the reception area because he hadn't recognized her at first glance. This was the pretty mother he remembered, and seeing her so happy after being sad and depressed for so long was the best feeling ever.

It felt like a new start for his mom, and he owed it all to Evie.

Evie was pleasant when he'd thanked her for fitting his mother into her schedule, and while she smiled on the outside as she accepted his credit card for payment and ran it through her system, the sentiment didn't fully reach her eyes. She continued to talk to his mother as if the two of them were now the best of friends, while keeping any conversation with him as short as possible.

Frustration welled inside him. He wanted to reach out and touch Evie, just to get some kind of real reaction from her. To see that familiar desire flare in her eyes, or her lips part longingly as she looked into his gaze and made him feel like he was all she needed to be happy. But that wasn't true, and since he had no right to put his hands on her, he kept them at his sides.

The makeover that Evie had given his mother was more than just a physical transformation. As he kept sneaking glances at his mother as he drove her home, he marveled at the smile on her glossy lips, the self-esteem that radiated off her, and the optimism that made him hopeful that this was a turning point in her life. A good, positive one.

But the closer they got to where his mother lived, the more her smile faded away. By the time they walked into the house, he felt a tangible, somber shift in her and wondered if his mom was already backsliding and immersing herself in the past again, in the memories that surrounded her on a daily basis.

He followed her into the kitchen, where she poured herself a glass of iced tea. "Mom . . . is everything okay?"

After taking a sip of her drink, she set the glass down on the counter and sighed before facing him. "No, everything isn't okay. I have some things I need to say to you. Things that should have been resolved a long time ago but I just wasn't ready to face reality. And that reality includes how I abandoned you after your sister died." Her voice cracked with emotion.

Eric sagged back against the counter, shocked by his mother's insight, but he wasn't sure he was ready to have this conversation with her. "Mom—"

"I haven't been a great mother the past thirteen years," she went on, ignoring his attempt to cut her off, clearly needing to get this off her chest. "And I know I hurt you with my indifference, while you've always been here for me, regardless of my depression, my grief, or my anger over losing Trisha."

"It was so hard for me, too, Mom," he said, his own throat raspy. "She was your daughter, but she was my sister and my twin and I lost such a big part of me when she died." He didn't need to dump everything on his mom or rehash things that would be painful, but she needed to know he'd been affected, too.

"I'm so sorry," she said, her voice contrite. "I think when I saw Patty at work, it made me realize everything I'd lost. Not just Trisha, but friendships I'd had for decades, your father, hobbies I once loved doing . . . and I knew if I didn't make changes, I could possibly lose you, too, because what reason would you have to stick around when I was taking more from you than you were getting in return? And the thought of us eventually drifting apart would completely devastate me."

Her anguish was real, and he closed the distance between them and pulled her into a hug. "I'm not going anywhere, Mom. Ever," he assured her, though he had to be honest with her, too. "But I don't want you living like this anymore. All your focus and energy on keeping Trisha's memories alive and making this house a shrine. She'll always be here with us, in ways that go beyond a memorial garden or all the pictures in the living room or keeping her bedroom the same as it was when she died." He remembered the butterfly at the lake, and how happy he'd been with that simple reminder of her. "Trisha would want you to move on and be happy."

His mother pulled back to look up at him, clutching his arms. "She'd want you to be happy, too."

It was on the tip of his tongue to say that he *was* happy, but considering how miserable he actually was without Evie, that would be a lie. He wasn't sure he'd ever again be as happy as he'd been with Evie last weekend.

"You love her, don't you?" his mother asked softly and more perceptively than she'd been the past thirteen years.

He had no idea what Evie and his mother had talked about at the salon, but clearly his mother had come to the conclusion that there was more between him and Evie than the friendship he'd told her. Again, it would be so easy to fudge the truth, but considering how open and honest his mother had just been with him, didn't he owe her the same courtesy?

"Yes . . ." The word sounded pained as it passed his lips. "As much as I know what it's like to love a woman, yes, I love her." Because the way he felt about her was a first for him.

"*You* don't need to know, Eric," his mother said, placing her hand on the left side of his chest. "Your *heart* knows, and it was just waiting for the right woman to come along."

He shook his head and moved back to the other side of the kitchen, not sure he was willing to leave it all up to his heart. "Did you know that as Trisha's fraternal twin, there is a shared risk of me getting cancer?"

"Yes. Trisha's doctor told us when she was diagnosed."

He exhaled a frustrated breath. "How is it fair to build a life and family with a woman when the possibility exists that I could die the same way?"

She blinked at him, taken aback by his question. "Eric, there are no guarantees for anyone in this life. You could die in a car accident tomorrow, the same way you could die of cancer or any other illness that's out of your control." She paused, then said, "You can't live your life second-guessing what is or isn't going to happen. You could be healthy for the rest of your life and live until you're ninety ... and if that happened and you never took a chance and built a life and family with a woman you love, would you have any regrets?"

He imagined the next sixty years without Evie in his life, and all he saw was a bleak, lonely future because no one would ever be able to replace her. He groaned and scrubbed a hand down his face.

"It's all fair if she knows and accepts the risks ahead of time, Eric," his mother went on gently. "And if you find a woman who is strong and tenacious enough to take that chance with you knowing what could possibly happen, then she's a woman worth fighting for. Don't push her out of your life because of unfounded fears, because Evie is the kind of girl that some other man is eventually going to snap up."

That thought made his gut churn with a shockingly possessive animosity, because he didn't want to share Evie with anyone. Ever. Because she was his and had been from the first time he'd laid eyes on her in the coffee shop.

What made him think, or even believe, he

could just let her go when she meant everything to him?

God, he'd been an idiot. So wrapped up in what he'd convinced himself was right over the years, he'd done just what she'd accused him of. Taken the choice away from her. Evie was right. His mom was right. Her being with him was her choice to make.

Now he just had to hope that he hadn't pushed her too far away.

ERIC COULD HAVE driven straight to Evie's place, but considering how badly he'd hurt her by rejecting the greatest gift anyone had ever given him—her love—she deserved flourish and fanfare. Hearts and flowers and bended knee. And that took at least a day to plan.

He shrugged into the black suit coat he'd brought with him to work to change into at the end of the day just as Leo strolled into his office. It had been a busy Friday, with their schedules conflicting, so his partner had no clue what Eric was up to.

Leo frowned at the dressy attire Eric was wearing. "What's with the suit and tie?" he asked. "Did I forget about an important meeting we had with a client tonight?"

"No." Eric adjusted the knot of his tie against the collar of his dress shirt and grinned at Leo. "I'm going to an awards dinner."

His confusion increased. "For?"

"To support my soon-to-be fiancée."

Understanding dawned across Leo's features. "Ahhh. You finally pulled your head out of your ass and realized that Evie is the best thing that has ever happened to you."

Eric couldn't even be irritated at Leo's comment, mainly because it was the truth. "Damn right I did. I'm going to go and get the girl and make her mine. The San Diego Chamber of Commerce is presenting her with this year's Humanitarian Award at tonight's dinner, and after that, well, we're going to go and celebrate our engagement."

"You sound pretty sure of yourself," Leo said, bracing his shoulder against the doorjamb. "There's usually groveling involved in this sort of thing to win the girl back. They love it when you grovel."

Eric laughed. "There will be a little groveling." He'd gladly get on his knees for Evie, for a variety of reasons.

"And don't forget about a grand gesture," Leo suggested helpfully. "Trust me, that's the clincher for women."

"Got it all covered," Eric assured his friend, feeling confident that he'd managed to achieve the wow factor for Evie.

Was he nervous about tonight and her reaction? Maybe a tiny bit, but deep down, he knew that Evie wasn't the kind of woman who would change her mind about her feelings for him overnight. She was tried and true, which was one of the things he loved about her.

He was the one who'd walked away from her. He was the one with the hang-ups and fears, but she'd already assured him that she wanted him, even knowing the risks. He'd be a fool to give up a lifetime with her over something that might never happen. Going forward, there would be no doubts, no unfounded fears, and no constant what-ifs overshadowing his feelings for her.

No, there would only be Evie and their life and future together, which was all that mattered to him.

"AND THIS YEAR'S humanitarian award goes to Evie Bennett for her Beautiful You program that supports the local women's domestic abuse shelters."

A round of applause broke out in the room where the Chamber of Commerce was hosting the awards dinner. Evie was one of the last recipients of the evening, and with Scarlett and Jessica sitting at the same table in support of Evie and her nomination, she scooted back her chair and made her way up to the podium in the little black dress she'd worn for the occasion.

She wasn't much of a public speaker, but she'd written a few notes so she didn't forget the key points of her thank-you speech, which was her biggest worry. Standing in front of the filled room with all eyes on her, she kept her gaze mostly on Jessica and Scarlett—who was taping the acceptance speech—as a focal point as she explained the Beautiful You program and why she'd created it. She talked about women's abuse issues, then thanked her partners at the salon for their time and donated products and the Chamber of Commerce for putting a spotlight on the Beautiful You program.

Another round of applause ensued, and as she picked up her award and started down the stairs from the podium, she caught sight of a man standing in the very back of the room in a black suit with his arms overflowing with at least two dozen long-stemmed red roses.

Shocked to see Eric, she felt her breath catch in her throat, and she faltered on her heels before regaining her balance and composure and did the only thing her heart was telling her to do. She didn't know why he was there, but she set her award on the table next to Scarlett, then kept walking straight toward Eric, trusting her instincts, trusting *him*, that he'd somehow, someway, come to his senses and was there to sweep her off her feet.

Please let him be here to sweep me off my feet.

It was a lot to ask for, but she wouldn't accept anything less from him.

She stopped a few feet away and nearly melted when he gave her one of his sexy, disarming smiles.

"I hear that grand gestures are a way to a woman's heart," he said, indicating the flowers he was holding, the gorgeous, deep red roses contrasting against his black suit.

Truly, there was only one way to *this* woman's heart. She didn't need her gestures to be grand, just heartfelt and real.

He looked into her eyes, narrowing this moment down to just the two of them, even though they were in a room with over one hundred other people watching Eric's grand gesture play out.

"So, you'll be happy to know that this is the part where I tell you what an idiot I was."

She bit back a smile, loving his sense of humor. "That's a good start."

"And that I won't be so stupid again."

"Debatable," she teased, and heard a few light laughs from the tables behind them.

His expression turned serious. "And that I want you in my life for a very long time, like *forever,* which is the nonnegotiable part of this grand gesture."

Hope and joy started pumping through her veins. "I'd like that, too," she whispered.

His gaze softened and he looked at her as though she was his sun and moon and stars. "And that I'm going to live my life to the fullest, each and every day, with you right by my side."

Her heart . . . Oh, God, her heart was nearly overflowing with happiness. "Okay," she agreed.

He went down on one knee in front of her,

causing most of the people in the room to gasp at the gallant gesture and where it was heading. Anticipation sped up Evie's pulse as he gave her the roses, then reached into the front pocket of his suit, retrieving a small, black velvet box.

"No more doubts. No more fears," he said, his voice strong and sure as he opened the lid, revealing a breathtaking engagement ring that nearly blinded her with its multifaceted sparkles. "I love you, Evie Bennett, and I won't settle for anything less than you marrying me so you can be mine for the rest of our lives."

Tears filled her eyes because she felt like the luckiest girl on the planet. And then she smiled because this man was proof that a girl had to kiss a few toads to find her prince. "Yes. I'll marry you."

He slipped the ring on her finger, then stood back up and kissed her, so soft and sweet and gentle, before literally sweeping her off her feet, roses and all, and into his arms. With the rest of the guests cheering, he carried her out to a limousine waiting by the curb, and once he had them locked inside, he pulled her across his lap and pressed her forehead to his.

"Thank you," he whispered.

"For what?"

"For not giving up on me while I was in my idiot phase," he said wryly.

She laughed. "Never," she promised, and she meant it.

EPILOGUE

Eight months later...

ERIC STOOD FACING the beautiful woman who was about to become his wife, holding both of her hands in his, and marveling at what a lucky man he was that Evie was going to be his for the rest of their lives together.

It was a beautiful spring afternoon in San Diego, and they'd opted to have the small wedding ceremony and reception in his mother's backyard. Evie had done most of the planning, and she'd explained that this is where he grew up with Trisha, and it was important that her memory was honored on their wedding day. His sister couldn't be there physically, but spiritually she would be in their hearts.

Sitting in the few rows of chairs behind them were only close friends and family. His mother, of course, who'd managed to rebuild friendships and was pursuing outside interests that kept her active and fulfilled. His father and his new wife had flown down from Arizona, and Evie's parents, her brother and Aaron, and her grandfather were present, as well. His partner and best friend, Leo, was there with his wife, along with Aiden and Daisy, and of course since Dylan was the reason why Eric had met Evie in the first place, he and his wife, Serena, were there to witness the nuptials, along with Scarlett and Jessica.

Evie had hired the same minister that had spoken at Trisha's memorial service to perform the wedding ceremony, replacing what had been a sad day almost fourteen years ago with a happy, celebratory one now. They stood beneath a small archway threaded with gorgeous white and pale pink flowers, but he couldn't take his eyes off of the woman who'd given his life new purpose.

She wore a simple white off-the-shoulder wedding gown. Her hair was loose and flowing around her shoulders, just how he liked it best, and her light blue eyes shone with tenderness and adoration as she promised to love, honor, and cherish him, until death did they part.

His heart squeezed tight in his chest. How had he gotten so damn lucky?

He slipped her wedding ring on her finger,

the minister announced them as husband and wife, and right in front of everyone he kissed the hell out of his bride until the small crowd behind them were clapping and whistling and cheering.

Holding her hand, they faced their standing guests. Before the ceremony, Eric had noticed that everyone had been given a small white box. He'd assumed it was a wedding favor of some sort, until his family and friends simultaneously lifted the lids and each box released a monarch butterfly.

Eric sucked in a breath as a dozen of them took flight, then glanced at his wife, who merely gave him a soft smile and said, "For Trisha."

Yes, for Trisha. Stunned by Evie's thoughtful gesture, and overwhelmed by the emotion that filled him to overflowing—which was pure joy and happiness—he watched as the butterflies fluttered around the backyard, then flew away ... all except one, which landed on the floral wrist corsage Evie had opted for over a bouquet. It didn't stay there long, but Eric felt his sister's presence with them.

Over the next few hours, they ate pepperoni and mushroom pizza with extra cheese, had cupcakes for dessert, and visited with everyone until Eric decided he wanted Evie all to himself.

They had a suite at the Ritz Carlton for the night, and the next day they were heading to Hawaii for a week long honeymoon. But for the next few hours, Eric planned to consummate the hell out of their marriage.

He sat on the bed in the hotel room waiting for Evie to emerge from the bathroom, and when she did a short while later, he groaned at how tempting she looked. She'd changed into a sweet cotton baby doll type nightie that was all white and edged in lace. As she walked toward him, the split of material in front parted ways, giving him a glimpse of matching white cotton panties with a simple pink bow on the waistband . . . and she was all his to unwrap and enjoy.

She stopped by her overnight bag and withdrew a long, flat box with a white bow wrapped around it. "I have a wedding gift for you," she said, and smiled as she crawled up onto the bed beside Eric and handed him the present.

He took the box, feeling bad that he hadn't reciprocated. "I didn't get you anything."

She rolled her eyes. "You've given me the best gift ever. First, by becoming my husband, and second . . . well, open the present and you'll see."

He wasn't sure what that meant, but he pulled off the ribbon and lifted the lid, confused at first at what he was looking at . . . a long, white plastic stick with an oval cut-out with the word YES and a plus sign next to it. He wasn't familiar with pregnancy tests, but as he lifted his gaze to Evie's and saw the soft, hopeful, loving look in her eyes, his heart started to race at the possibility.

He swallowed hard, trying to hold his excitement at bay until he had confirmation. "Is this . . . are you . . . are we having a baby?"

She bit her bottom lip and nodded. "Yes, we are."

"Evie," he breathed in disbelief, because being a dad was something he'd never thought would happen for him before this woman had completely changed his life and his vision for their future. And yes, that included babies. A family of their own. "You're really pregnant?"

"Yes," she laughed, and moved over onto him so that she was straddling Eric's thighs and facing him. She cupped his face in her hands. "I know we talked about waiting a while to have kids, but it must have happened when I switched out my birth control a few months back. I'm about eight weeks along."

He smirked at her. "It must have been my Grade A Prime beef," he teased as he slid his hands up along her thighs and around to squeeze her ass in his palms.

She giggled as she brushed her lips across his. "God, you're so dirty."

"You love it." He dragged her closer, so she could *feel* that Grade A Prime beef pressing insistently against the crux of her thighs. "It's why you married me."

"Partly, yes," she admitted, and stared into his eyes, right to his very soul. "But it's because I love you more. You're going to be an amazing dad. You got this."

She said it with such tenderness and conviction, but he wasn't going to lie. The thought of becoming a father and taking care of another human life was a little bit terrifying. But knowing he had this incredible woman by his side, who brought out the best in him every single day, he knew without a doubt they were going to rock this whole parent thing.

"No, *we* got this," he amended, because they were now a team. "Together."

She pressed her lips to his, smiling against his mouth. "Yes, we do," she agreed. "Always together."

Thank you for reading THE BOYFRIEND EXPERIENCE. We hope you enjoyed Eric and Evie's story! We would appreciate it if you would help others enjoy this book by leaving a review at your preferred e-tailer. Thank you!

Don't miss Leo, Dylan, and Aiden's stories in the Tall, Dark & Sexy Series!
TALL, DARK & CHARMING
TALL, DARK AND IRRESISTIBLE
TALL, DARK AND TEMPTING

Read Carly's super sexy Knight Brothers Series!

All alpha all the time, Sebastian Knight's confidence never wavers. At least not until Ashley Easton walks back into his life, wanting nothing to do with the playboy who broke her heart.

Sebastian Knight is a closer. Be it a business deal or the woman of his choice, everything he wants is his for the taking. Sexy and irresistible, a wink, a smile, or a handshake always seals the deal. Until Ashley returns at the worst possible time, and everything unravels around him.

The Ashley who returns is sassy and sexy—everything Sebastian craves and he wants a second chance. Despite her reluctance, his sex appeal makes it harder and harder to keep him at arm's length.

Sebastian might have a talent for sealing the deal, but Ashley is no longer easily charmed. This time he's going to have to work to win.

Sign up for Carly Phillips & Erika Wilde's Newsletters:

Carly's Newsletter
http://smarturl.it/CarlysNewsletter

Erika's Newsletter
http://smarturl.it/ErikaWildeNewsletter

About the Authors

Carly Phillips

Carly Phillips is the *N.Y. Times* and *USA Today* Bestselling Author of over 50 sexy contemporary romance novels featuring hot men, strong women and the emotionally compelling stories her readers have come to expect and love. Carly is happily married to her college sweetheart, the mother of two nearly adult daughters and three crazy dogs (two wheaten terriers and one mutant Havanese) who star on her Facebook Fan Page and website. Carly loves social media and is always around to interact with her readers. You can find out more about Carly at www.carlyphillips.com.

Erika Wilde

Erika Wilde is the author of the sexy Marriage Diaries series and The Players Club series. She lives in Oregon with her husband and two daughters, and when she's not writing you can find her exploring the beautiful Pacific Northwest. For more information on her upcoming releases, please visit website at www.erikawilde.com.

FEB 2 8 2020

2-27-20
1-24-22
12
0